ELIZA PROKOPOVITS

Her Cursed Apple

Copyright © 2023 by Eliza Prokopovits

All rights reserved. No part of this publication may be reproduced, stored or transmitted in any form or by any means, electronic, mechanical, photocopying, recording, scanning, or otherwise without written permission from the publisher. It is illegal to copy this book, post it to a website, or distribute it by any other means without permission.

First edition

*This book was professionally typeset on Reedsy.
Find out more at reedsy.com*

Contents

Chapter 1	1
Chapter 2	9
Chapter 3	19
Chapter 4	25
Chapter 5	34
Chapter 6	40
Chapter 7	50
Chapter 8	57
Chapter 9	66
Chapter 10	74
Chapter 11	82
Chapter 12	90
Chapter 13	99
Chapter 14	109
Chapter 15	119
Chapter 16	129
Chapter 17	138
Chapter 18	149
Chapter 19	159
Chapter 20	172
Chapter 21	181
Chapter 22	190
Chapter 23	194
Chapter 24	201

Chapter 25	210
Chapter 26	223
Her Enchanted Tower: Chapter 1	233
Also By Eliza Prokopovits	241
About the Author	242

Chapter 1

Winston's mouth dropped open in horror. Bianca ignored him, scooting further into the hollow beneath the fallen trees that had fit them so much better when they were younger. She settled across from him, her knees in her lightweight cotton riding habit pressing against his. Her friend had shot up like a weed a few years ago, and now his tall, lanky frame was the main reason they were outgrowing their childhood hideout.

Still ignoring Winston's scowl, only somewhat hidden by the dark blond curls that tumbled over his forehead and blue eyes, she pulled a napkin of stolen honey almond biscuits from her pocket and unwrapped them, offering him one.

"Bribes won't work," he grumbled. "It's gone too far."

Bianca glared at him, daring him to say another word, to say that her clandestine pugilism lessons needed to end. He'd said it enough times over the past six years that she knew exactly what was coming.

Rather than squirming under her glare like he used to, Winston leaned forward, his frown both earnest and regretful. "This one's worse than the last," he said, his eyes perusing her face where a puffy, purplish bruise graced her cheekbone and partially obscured her right eye.

"It was an accident." Bianca shrugged. "Any fighter has to be prepared to take a few hits. I'm not hurt, nor am I frightened to be hurt in the future."

"But you're *not* a fighter," Winston protested. "You're a young lady, and if I'm to have any hope of being a man of honor, I can't raise a fist against you anymore. I—"

"Should have stopped years ago, I know," Bianca sighed. "You've told me. A hundred times."

After a brief silence, Winston said, "What tale did you spin this time?"

"No need. Papa is still in town, and the servants all generously pretend not to know what I get up to. Nurse tutted over me a bit, but she looks the other way even better than everyone else." Bianca's smile was a little crooked because of her puffy eye, but it was genuine. She loved Nurse, who had been the nearest thing she'd had to a mother for most of her life.

Relaxing slightly, she took a bite of one biscuit and offered the other to Winston again. He sighed and took it, studying it broodingly for a moment before swallowing the whole thing in two bites.

Bianca couldn't help remembering the first time they'd had this same conversation. She'd been nine; Winston had been just starting his proper lessons with his new tutor at age twelve. One of his lessons had been pugilism, and he'd promised to teach her everything he learned, but he'd accidentally given her a black eye during their first practice and refused to teach her more. She *had* needed to lie to Papa about that one. She'd claimed that her horse Diamond had spooked and run, and she'd hit her face on a branch. To her dismay, Papa had insisted a groom accompany her on her rides.

She glanced out of the tree cave toward where Harry

stood with the horses. Who knew that the groom her father had assigned to her was a former bare-knuckle boxer and prizefighter? He'd agreed to give them both lessons in the interest of saving their friendship after he overheard Bianca threatening to never speak to Winston again if he went back on his promise. It had been six years, and Bianca secretly thought that they were probably both good enough to go a round with any prizefighter in England. And Harry had become more a friend and teacher than a servant by now.

"Has your father written to say when he'll arrive home?"

"Three weeks. They hoped to hold the wedding before the end of the Season and all their potential guests left town."

"Late May is cutting it close. Mother and I weren't the only ones who left at the end of April."

Bianca shrugged. "I guess that was the soonest she could be ready. My new stepmother." She said the word with trepidation, testing it, tasting it to see if it would be bitter or sweet. When she was younger, she often wished for a mother, a warm, loving figure to fill the void left by the one she could barely remember. She had wished for siblings, too—younger brothers and sisters to fill Eston Hall and provide playmates for those rainy days when she couldn't ride out to meet Winston in the woods. Now, though, she was fifteen, and she no longer needed a playmate. She would be grown and married and moved away before any child born to her stepmother would even be old enough for the schoolroom. And she had a houseful—two houses, if she counted Winston's family at Pinehurst—of people willing to love her. She didn't much see the need for a stepmother anymore. Of course, Papa was not terribly old—nearing fifty wasn't nearing death—and he was well within his rights to want a wife and a male heir for the Viscount of Eston title.

Bianca could feel Winston's gaze on her, but he remained silent. They'd discussed all of this when she'd received her father's first letter informing her that he was courting. In all the years he'd gone to town for the sitting of Parliament, this was the first he'd participated in all the social events of the London Season. It had taken a full week of conversations with eminently rational Winston for Bianca to come to terms with it. Thankfully, Papa's first letter had arrived on the heels of Winston's own return from town after spending a fortnight there with his parents. She might have combusted from the confusion of feelings without her friend to talk them through. It had been such a shock that she had barely complained about being left behind and missing out on the sights of London—again.

"Did he tell you any more about her?" Winston asked finally.

Bianca shrugged. "Her name is Malorie Franklin. She's seven-and-twenty and remarkably pretty."

"Then why hasn't she married yet? If she's pretty, you would think someone would have taken her off the market after her first Season or two."

"He didn't say, but it's probably something about her fortune, isn't it? Papa would never care about that, but others might."

Winston nodded. He studied her for a minute, his brow furrowing. "Bee? What else did he say?"

Bianca sighed, wishing her friend couldn't read her so easily. "Nothing, really, only that he thinks she'll be just what we need to prepare me for my entrance into society." A tremor of nerves rippled through her stomach. With her coming out not expected for another three years, she had planned to go on as she was and only start worrying about pleasing the *ton*

CHAPTER 1

when the time got closer. Her father and her new stepmother, however, might have other ideas. Somehow she knew that even if she adored this Malorie Franklin—she'd be Malorie Snow by then—her life was about to change in uncomfortable ways.

Winston made a noncommittal but supportive noise. Before he could comment, however, Harry appeared at the entrance of their little hideout.

"Time to be riding back, Miss Snow. You promised to devote some of the afternoon to history, remember."

Bee sighed and dragged herself out of the cave with Winston on her heels. Nurse wasn't a strict schoolmistress by any means, but Bianca would much rather spend her days riding and boxing than studying. She liked reading well enough on rainy days, but the May weather was too beautiful to waste.

"I'll bring you a new spell tomorrow," Winston offered.

"A good one?"

"Naturally."

She rewarded him with a bright smile. He grinned. She joined Harry and Diamond at the stump that served as a mounting block. Once she was in the saddle, the other two mounted. She and Harry turned toward home with a final wave to Winston, who rode off in the other direction toward Pinehurst.

Eston Hall was a large, whimsical stone house that had begun existence over a century ago at half the size and had been expanded over the years by throwing out a wing here and a garret there. It sat in the middle of a large park with fields, forest, and a large pond perfect for boating. The Viscounts of Eston had lived there for the last three generations. Their neighbors, the Earls of Rowland, had built Pinehurst even earlier, and while the current earl—Winston's father—jovially teased Bianca's father about settling a little close for comfort, nobody actually minded the proximity. The forest that stretched between the houses gave plenty of privacy, and it had provided endless hours of exploration and amusement for Bianca and Winston, who had been inseparable from the moment they'd been allowed to run loose on the estates. Despite the approach of adulthood, no one had tried to curtail their adventures, as long as Harry rode along to ensure Bee's safety.

***

Fortunately, Bianca's black eye had returned to normal by the time her father returned home with his new bride. She didn't ride out to meet Winston on the day they were due to arrive, wanting to stay close to home so that she'd be ready and waiting as soon as the carriage rolled up the drive. She was always eager to see Papa after he'd been gone for three months to London, but there was an extra anticipation and apprehension that had her fidgeting in her seat while a maid pinned up her hair. What would her stepmother see when she looked at her? Bee studied herself in the mirror. Hair so dark it was nearly black and so straight it would barely hold a curl, and dark brown eyes to match. Pale skin that refused to gain a golden glow no matter how much she was out in the sun, but at least it didn't freckle. Pink cheeks and rosy lips completed the picture. Her day dress was dark blue and simple, not the latest style but tidy and neatly pressed. At a glance, no one would guess that she'd sported a purplish-green trophy from a sparring match only a week ago, or that she shirked

CHAPTER 1

her lessons as often as she could get away with it, or that she made a game of stealing sweets from the kitchen. Bee smiled at her reflection. This was exactly the first impression she was aiming for.

It was another two hours before the carriage rolled up in front of the house, and Bianca spent the time pacing the drawing room. The book she was supposed to be reading—a tedious biography of Charlemagne—lay untouched on the side table alongside a tepid cup of tea. At the sight of the familiar carriage, she hurried to the entrance hall, where she was joined by Nurse and Mrs. Portman, the housekeeper, and a lineup of servants. Nerves fluttered through Bee's chest as Hawke, the butler, opened the door, and two figures entered the hall. The woman clinging to Papa's arm was tallish and lovely: glossy chestnut curls, primrose cheeks, amber eyes. Her lips were red and full, and she was smiling nervously. Her dress was the color of fresh peaches, and it made her glow in the light from the windows. Bee tried to reconcile this fine lady with her long-held daydream of a mother and couldn't. Somehow the knowledge that her new stepmother was only twelve years her senior hadn't quite settled in until they stood face to face. They were practically of an age to be sisters. So she gaped, speechless, as the last lingering hope she'd unknowingly held of having a real mother and a mother's love winked out of existence.

Then Papa stepped forward and said Bee's name, breaking her from her thoughts, and she ran to him, flinging herself into his arms. He swept her up and spun her around, laughing.

"I missed you, Papa," she said softly, so that only he could hear.

"I missed you, too, my little snowflake." His dark eyes

sparkled, and he kissed her cheek. Setting her feet on the floor, he turned to the woman who waited hesitantly a few steps behind. "Bianca, I want you to meet Malorie Snow, Lady Eston."

Bianca swept her best curtsy and met Malorie's shy smile with one of her own. "Welcome, my lady. We're so glad you're here." It might not be the complete truth, but Bee would try to make it so, for her father's sake. The new viscountess might not be the mother she'd subconsciously hoped for, but she decided she could make do with a sister. She'd never had one of those either, and perhaps she'd like that just as well.

Malorie's smile widened slightly, and she curtsied as well. "I'm delighted to meet you, Bianca. Your father talks about you a great deal."

Bee shot Papa a sidelong glance, hoping he hadn't described all her childhood scrapes. She'd gotten into countless, but those were best not spoken of.

"Only the good things, love," Papa murmured with a wink.

Bee relaxed, until she caught the slight lift of Malorie's eyebrows. She stifled a sigh. Papa's comment would only serve to suggest that there were not so good things to tell as well. There went her positive first impression.

Bianca stepped back as Papa introduced Malorie to Mrs. Portman and the rest of the staff then led her up the stairs to the room adjoining his that had been prepared for her. Once they had left the entrance hall, Bee's shoulders slumped, and she hurried up the back stairs to her own room to change into a riding habit. Winston wouldn't be waiting for her, but she needed a good gallop across the park to clear her head.

Chapter 2

Malorie stood by the window in her room and took a deep breath. Her trunk had just been delivered, and Lord Eston had left her to freshen up after the long drive. But instead of finding a gown for dinner, Malorie gazed out at the green countryside. So this was her new home. It fully satisfied her expectations—in many ways, exceeded them. It was a large, comfortable house in a fine park. There were enough servants that she wouldn't have to lift a finger if she didn't want to, and those that she'd met so far had seemed eager to please.

It was just strange, this drastic life change. Did every new bride go through feelings like these? Yesterday she'd been merely Miss Franklin, on the frightening verge of becoming a spinster, living in a modest townhouse near Mayfair. Today she was Lady Eston, a viscountess.

The changes in her life weren't bad in any respect. She'd always dreamed of finding a wealthy husband, ideally a titled one, and she'd succeeded. And despite Lord Eston being nearly twice her age—he'd admitted to turning eight-and-forty last fall—he was still a very handsome man. The sprinkling of silver in his dark hair lent an air of distinction to his rather dashing good looks. In truth, she'd felt light enough to float away when he'd first asked her for a dance. He'd been kind and courteous and alluringly interested in her.

Being married to this man would be no hardship.

Suddenly having a daughter, on the other hand, would take getting used to, particularly one who wasn't so very much younger than herself. The girl had looked at her with wide, dark eyes so like her father's, and her gaze had been bright and curious. She would be no insipid miss. Lord Eston had assured his daughter that he'd only told the good things, and she wondered now what stories he hadn't shared.

Motion out the window caught her eye, and Malorie saw the young woman on a gray mare, cantering along a path through the fields, trailed by a groom on a dark bay. Her hair had come loose from its earlier pins and flew out behind her, and she raised her hatless head to the sun. It was a charmingly rustic picture, but it cemented Malorie's guess that the girl was a hoyden. Lord Eston surely knew this; he had been careful not to frighten his new bride away.

Well. Malorie didn't know how to rein in the wild girl, but she'd find a way. And she'd have to do it soon, if they were to have any hope of presenting the young lady in town in a few years. Now that she was Lady Eston, Bianca's behavior reflected on Malorie as well as her father.

***

Bianca was dressed, breakfasted, and doing her lessons in the schoolroom by the time the new Lady Eston emerged from her rooms the next morning. Bee knew that town hours were different than country hours—Winston had told her when he'd first gone to London with his parents several years ago that

CHAPTER 2

all the adults stayed up half the night and slept in sometimes until noon—but Papa had never struggled to adjust back to rising early. Perhaps it was harder when it was one's first time. Malorie seemed like the type of person who had lived in cities for most of her life.

A short while later, her stepmother stopped by the schoolroom with Mrs. Portman. The housekeeper had been showing her around the house, reintroducing her to the staff and getting her acquainted with the running of Eston Hall. Bianca and Nurse had both been introduced yesterday, but Bee watched Nurse's reintroduction curiously over the treatise on mathematics she was supposed to be studying. Of course, Bee had known that Nurse had a name, but she'd been calling her Nurse for so long that it felt strange to hear the dear woman introduced as Sylvia Smith.

"You're the nurse?" Malorie was saying with a frown, as if she'd missed that fact on their first introduction. After the long drive from town and the overwhelm of a whirlwind wedding and move to the country, she could probably be pardoned for not catching every detail upon her arrival at her new home.

"Been with the family since Miss Snow was born, milady." Nurse bobbed another small curtsy.

"Where is her governess?"

"No governess, milady. I've been overseeing Miss Snow's education." Bee noticed a hint of pink in Nurse's cheeks.

A crease formed between Malorie's brows. "I see. And what has she learned?"

"She has a solid grasp of mathematics and literature, milady, as well as history, and she excels at geography."

"What about accomplishments?"

"Milady?"

"Have you taught her music?"

"No, milady. Nor dancing. I never learned those myself."

"Hmm. Magic?"

Nurse shook her head.

"The modern languages?"

"No, milady."

"Drawing?"

"We tried that, milady, without much success."

Bianca, listening, cringed. Their experiment with drawing had gone abysmally. She could admit to herself that she had absolutely no aptitude for art, but that didn't mean she liked her deficiencies listed out so comprehensively.

"Has she been taught anything about running a household?"

"Yes, milady," Mrs. Portman spoke up. "She's been learning everything I could teach her for years."

"Good. But what about planning and hosting a ball or a house party?"

"No, milady."

Bee blinked from behind her book. Were those things expected? Her father often invited neighboring families over for dinner while he was home, but their table never sat more than eight, though it could fit more. Bee had no experience even attending larger events, let alone hosting them, and she barely had a wide enough acquaintance for the few social engagements they had.

Malorie pursed her lips and tutted. "This situation won't do. I must engage a proper governess at once. My lord ought to have engaged one years ago. Bianca will have to work extra hard, or she'll be behind all the other young ladies in accomplishments when she comes out."

Bianca stared at her, aghast. Even Mrs. Portman looked

surprised.

"That seems drastic, milady. Surely no harm has been done by the delay."

"Lady Petersham's daughters are only eight, and they've been taking lessons in magic and music for the past six months." Malorie cast her gaze over Bianca, who quickly lowered her eyes to her book. "Hiring a governess will be my first priority. When she comes, Miss Smith, your services will no longer be required until our family increases."

Bee scowled at the pages in front of her, barely seeing the words. Nurse would be dismissed as soon as the new governess took up residence, unless Malorie was expecting a baby. While Bianca had given up on wishing for younger siblings, she suddenly hoped for a baby so that Nurse could stay. She didn't need a nurse any longer, and she liked the idea of having proper magic lessons from a governess rather than second-hand instruction from Winston. But while Malorie might see Nurse as staff, to Bianca, she was family.

***

"She's sending Nurse away and hiring a governess."

Winston looked up as Bianca swung herself down from her saddle. He could see at a glance how upset she was. Bee had always been one for big emotions that showed in every line of her body.

He finished feeding Grayling the last chunk of carrot then wiped his hands on his breeches, crossing to Bee as Harry took Diamond's reins from her. She looked about ready to start swinging her fists if only a suitable target presented itself, but Winston could see the deeper hurt, so he risked injury by pulling her into a hug. They used to comfort each other like this after many a childhood scrape, but they hadn't so much in recent years. Bee had decided, once she'd learned to take out her feelings through boxing, that she had no further need of cuddles or comfort. She probably had no idea that Winston had stopped for an entirely different reason. He liked the feel of his best friend in his arms far too much to risk the delightful torment often.

But she needed a hug now, and he felt justified in his choice as she leaned into him and laid her head against his collarbone with a soft sigh. He rested his cheek against her hair, smelling soap and summer sun on the raven-dark strands.

"I know Nurse gave you the only mothering you've ever known, but she's not the only person who loves you, Bee."

She straightened and pulled back, leaving Winston wishing he hadn't broken the moment. Bee was blinking hard as if fending off tears, and he wanted to pull her back into his arms. But she shook her head and said lightly, teasing, "Of course not. I'm the most popular person in the parish and the darling of two estates. Even *your* parents like me best."

Winston chuckled, loving her bravado as much as her vulnerability. "Naturally, they do."

She sighed heavily, the lightness falling. "I'm going to miss her."

"Of course you will. If it helps, you got to keep her longer than I did. Remember, Nanny was replaced by Mr. Turbot when I was twelve."

"The reprieve only means that now I'll have to catch up on years of the most awful lessons." Bee stormed away from him across the clearing, all her agitation returning. "It's just not fair that Malorie can come in and take over and immediately wreck my life."

"That's maybe a bit dramatic." Though it wasn't surprising that Bee felt that way. Her stepmother had been with them for less than a full day, and she was already making changes. Winston shoved his hands into his pockets. "She *is* your father's wife, and we expected her to prepare you for your introduction to society."

She rounded on him, pointing a finger for emphasis. "You should have heard her, Winston. She expects me to learn music and drawing and dancing and languages and hostessing and… and…" She threw her hands up. "I am apparently less accomplished than an eight year old." She crossed her arms and glowered.

One corner of Winston's mouth twitched up. Even her petulance was adorable. "I highly doubt that." He leaned against the trunk of a nearby tree. "You're well read, you can do magic nearly as well as I can, and you know more about geography than anyone I've ever met."

Bee rolled her eyes, obviously in no mood to be mollified.

Winston tried again. "The rest is mostly frippery, to impress the *ton*. All the young ladies learn these things and show them off during their Seasons."

"If you think for one moment, Winston Elliot Graham, that I care a jot for dancing at balls or drinking tea in stuffy drawing rooms with self-important strangers, then you're an idiot."

The grin he'd been suppressing stretched wide across his face. He used to hate when she was annoyed enough at him to bring out his full name, but now he just loved her fierceness. "But you *do* want to go to London."

Bee sighed. "I do."

It had been a sore point for years that her father left her

behind when he went to town for Parliament. She'd been told that she'd be miserably bored in town and that she was much better off in the country with Diamond and the woods and gardens. This may have been true, but it didn't stop Winston from feeling guilty every year when his mother took him along for a few weeks.

"I just want to *see* it all. Westminster and St. Paul's, the Tower, the Exchange, Elgin's Marbles…"

"And the only way they'll take you for a Season when you're eighteen is if they think you're ready for the Marriage Mart." He cringed at the final two words, but controlled his expression quickly. There was nothing he hated more than the idea of Bianca being on the market. But this conversation wasn't about what *he* wanted. "So the best way to get what you want is…" He gestured for her to finish the sentence.

Bee scowled and said nothing.

"To study hard and learn whatever your governess teaches you," he finished for her.

"But I don't *want* to get married. From what I can see, a husband would want me to stay at home and raise children, and I'd never get to see anything of the world. My life would be just as limited, only in a different house."

I wouldn't. Winston gulped back the words that would give away his true feelings. She wasn't ready to hear them. He said, carefully, "The right husband would do everything in his power to make your dreams come true, Bee. But I'm not suggesting you have to accept any suitors. I'm simply saying that to get your wish of seeing London, you need to—"

"Do what Malorie wants me to," she sighed.

He gave her a sympathetic smile. "Some of your lessons might be fun—you might find you enjoy music or dancing, and you already like magic. And learning French and Italian would set you up well for a Grand Tour someday."

Bee's expression softened. He knew he'd scored a point. She didn't just want to see London; she wanted to see everything, everywhere.

"And," Winston added, stepping toward her and reaching out to touch her crossed arms, gently coaxing them out of their knot so that he could take her hands, "when you have your Season, I'll come to town and show you all my favorite places."

"But you'll be at Oxford still, won't you?"

"If I am, I'll ride to London every weekend for the entire term."

"Promise?"

To claim her time for himself to the exclusion of other men? "With all my heart." He squeezed her hands gently before letting go.

Bianca dropped her gaze from his, a small frown still creasing her brow. He could see her coming to terms with the situation, accepting that she'd have to learn what she could from whatever governess her new stepmother hired because, for now, their goals aligned. The tension hadn't left her shoulders, however.

Winston reached out and tapped a finger against the back of her wrist. "Want to hit something?"

"So badly."

He grinned. This was why he kept sparring with her even when he knew he shouldn't. He'd do anything to ease her irritation and bring her smile back. "For my personal safety, it's probably best if you work out your frustration on a target that isn't my face. What do you think, Harry?" He raised his voice to call the last question over his shoulder.

"Right you are, Master Graham." Harry grinned as he pulled an old shawl from his saddlebag and wrapped it around his hand to serve as Bianca's target. He'd been doing this since her very first boxing lessons so she could learn the skills without either of the two friends injuring each other.

Winston looked on as they took their places.

"Hands up, Miss Snow," Harry coached. "Always protect yourself."

Chapter 3

Malorie was as good as her word. Within a month, Nurse was packing to leave, and the new governess was expected to arrive any day. Malorie welcomed the new governess in the drawing room alone. If Bee had still been a child of ten, she would have hung over the banister in hopes of glimpsing the woman. Instead, she walked the gardens behind the house, trying to be patient through her growing apprehension. She couldn't help wondering what dreadful things Malorie was saying as the conference seemed to stretch on for hours.

Not that her stepmother disliked her, or at least, she didn't think so. But the new viscountess definitely disapproved. Each night at dinner, she corrected Bee's posture, how she held her spoon, the size of the bites she took, how long to chew and swallow before speaking, whether to speak at the table at all. Suddenly the time Bee had loved most—the time she'd always shared with her father—was turning into the activity she most wished to avoid.

Dinner wasn't the only time Malorie was critical. Bee was allowed to go riding, but never alone, and only at a sedate walk, a trot at most. She was used to having Harry along, of course, and they relaxed the rules as soon as they were out of sight of the house. She loved cantering across the back fields. Malorie insisted that Bee not leave the house without a bonnet—protection from the sun in good weather, protection from rain in wet. Bee only fought the command once. Lady Eston declared that if Bianca would not wear a bonnet, she would not set foot out of doors, and wearing the dratted hat was better than being cooped up inside.

Now Bee tugged on the bonnet strings tied snuggly under her chin but not hard enough to release the bow. She needed to look like a presentable young lady when she met the new governess if she was to make any sort of decent first impression.

"Bianca, dear," Malorie's musical voice said from behind her. "Come and meet Miss Hilton."

Bianca slowly turned, her heart seeming to beat in her throat. Her stepmother and the governess glided toward her along the garden path, barely seeming to notice the flame-colored rose bushes they passed. She curtsied. "It's a pleasure to meet you, Miss Hilton." She risked a glance at the woman who came to a halt beside Malorie.

Miss Hilton was older than Papa but younger than Nurse. She was trim and small, with a stiff spine and a prim expression. Her gray hair was in a simple knot at the nape of her neck, and her gray eyes evaluated Bee with cool intelligence.

"She's not the worst case I've handled." Miss Hilton addressed Malorie as if Bee weren't standing there. "We'll find her potential, I'm certain."

"Good." Malorie looked ready to dust her hands of the situation. "Lessons will begin tomorrow morning after breakfast. Bianca, please show Miss Hilton to her room."

Bee gave Malorie a pleading look. Her stepmother raised an

CHAPTER 3

eyebrow. Bee pasted on a gracious smile and led the governess into the house and up the stairs to the schoolroom. She paused just inside the doorway. A table stood along one wall, set with two chairs, and the spinet from the back parlor had been moved to rest against another wall. Two bedrooms opened off of the former nursery: Bee's on one side and Nurse's—now Miss Hilton's—on the other. Bee's door was closed, but the other bedroom stood open and empty. There was a bed, a desk, a washstand, and a wardrobe, of course, but the hand-stitched quilt that usually lay over Nurse's bed was gone, and the miniatures of Nurse's parents that had sat on the desk were gone as well. It was just a room. It bore no sign that a grandmotherly woman had lived there for fifteen years.

The next morning, Miss Hilton met Bianca in the schoolroom just as a maid brought up a breakfast tray with enough food for the two of them to share.

"I thought we could begin over breakfast by discussing what you've learned."

"Didn't my stepmother tell you?" Bee had not intended to be rude, but in her surprise at the unexpected question, the words blurted out.

"She did," Miss Hilton said in her prim manner, taking a seat at the table and pouring tea, "but I would like to hear from your perspective as well."

They had soon settled that Bee knew nothing about music or dancing or any language other than English.

"And what about drawing? Painting?"

"Horrendous," Bee admitted bluntly. "I have no aptitude for art at all."

"Hmm," considered Miss Hilton. "We'll try a few beginner lessons and see how we do."

Miss Hilton seemed to approve of Bianca's grasp of history and literature. "I was afraid I'd find a young lady who read nothing but gothic novels."

Bee shrugged. "I only have access to what's in the shop in town or what Papa brings home for me from London. I prefer reading travels and journals, anyway."

This led to a discussion of geography, which was by far Bianca's favorite subject. She was slightly behind in mathematics, and she had learned no natural science at all.

"And what of magic?"

Bee brightened. Here was another area in which she excelled. "I've learned quite a lot of the basics, plus a few advanced spells."

"Could you demonstrate, please?"

Bee obliged by lighting and snuffing the nearest candle with a murmured spell-word. Then she froze the dregs of tepid tea in her cup and melted it again. Finally, she levitated the book she'd been reading—the recently published narrative of the exploration across America by Meriwether Lewis and William Clark, which Papa had bought for her in town—so that it floated a few inches off the table before lowering back down with a soft thud.

Miss Hilton studied her for a moment. "Surprising. And very well done. Am I to assume you have learned no illusions?"

Bee frowned. "No. Should I have?"

A slight smile curved up the governess's lips. "Ladies are taught primarily illusions, Miss Snow, once they progress beyond candle lighting and the like. Who have you been learning from?"

"Winston," she said. At Miss Hilton's raised brows, she blushed. "Winston Graham, the son of Lord Rowland of Pinehurst. He's been teaching me magic ever since he began his own lessons."

"And how long has that been?"

"Six years."

"I see." She shook her head. "Well, a child teaching a child is not how I would have wished to begin your education in such a finicky subject, but I cannot deny that you have excellent control. We will skip over the basics, then, and proceed with illusions."

After several dozen more questions, Miss Hilton glanced at the clock. "It looks like we have our work cut out for us. The morning is half gone, but we will work on mathematics until lunch. Afterward, we will have your first music lesson."

The thought of mathematics until lunch was enough to make Bee's heart sink in horror, and the actual practice of it did not improve her opinion. She'd hoped that the music lesson would involve the spinet, but instead she was given sheets of music and shown how to read it. The notes spun in her vision, as if she'd somehow combined reading and mathematics into some bizarre third language that ought to translate into something beautiful but only made her head hurt.

After an hour of this, Miss Hilton released her for the afternoon. "Walking about in the sun will refresh you to study again tomorrow."

Bee had no intention of merely walking about. She changed into her riding habit faster than ever, shoving her feet into her boots and tying on her bonnet as she hurried to the stable. Harry looked up as if he'd been expecting her and began saddling Diamond without her saying a word. While he prepared the horses, she buttoned her boots.

"Keep to a walk, Miss Snow," Harry cautioned as they rode out of the stable yard.

With effort, Bee kept her pace slow. She wanted nothing more than to gallop. Between the frustration of the morning and the knowledge that Winston had probably been waiting an hour if he hadn't gone home already, she wished she could fly. Instead, she walked Diamond until the house was behind a low hill, and she could break into a canter.

Winston was waiting, but as they approached, he moved away from his horse as though he'd been about to leave.

"I thought you weren't coming," he said, coming to hold Diamond's head as Bee dismounted.

"Governess arrived yesterday." She didn't bother to suppress her scowl. "I had my first lessons with her today."

"Is she that bad?"

Bee hesitated, then shrugged. "Miss Hilton seems nice enough, but her list of things I need to learn is endless." She flopped onto her back on the pine-needle-cushioned forest floor and untied the strings of her bonnet.

Winston sat on the ground beside her. "Buck up," he said. "You're smart—you'll pick them up quickly. And remember that these lessons are your ticket to seeing London."

Bee nodded, clinging to the hope not only of exploring town but of seeing it all with Winston. His promise to show her the best sites might be the only thing that could get her through another day of lessons.

Chapter 4

By the end of her third day of lessons, Bee wasn't sure even a promise of exploring London was enough. Now that Miss Hilton knew exactly how much Bee didn't know, she'd drawn up a strict schedule for each day. They began with magic, then natural science, mathematics, and French.

"We'll begin Italian once I feel you have a reasonable grasp of French," she said.

Music followed, with or without the spinet, then drawing. If her lack of artistic skill weren't bad enough, Bee discovered that learning about composition and media was as dull as algebra.

When she'd finished her lessons on Friday afternoon, she changed to go riding like she did every day, but her father's voice stopped her as she passed his study.

"Come in a minute, snowflake," he said. "Close the door."

Bee obeyed, pushing the door closed behind her. Papa sat with his elbows on his desk, his hands clasped in front of him. His hair was the same raven's wing shade as her own, but his was lightly sprinkled with silver. She had his dark eyes, too, and fair skin. If she'd been a boy, she'd have been his spitting image.

She didn't mind—she'd always thought Papa handsome—but she'd often wished for some part of her to look like her mother, something she could look at in the mirror and say, *there, that's her*. Mama had died when Bianca was four, within hours of giving birth to a younger sister who hadn't survived the night. Most of Bee's recollections of her mother were vague: a cool hand on her forehead, a soft brush of lips on her cheek and the scent of lilac, a gentle voice singing her to sleep. And she couldn't be sure whether those muddled memories were of her mother or of Nurse. There was a portrait of the late viscountess on the wall behind Papa's chair. When she was younger, Bee used to sneak in while Papa was in town and sit with her back against the leg of his desk and just drink in the image of her mother. She was beautiful, with rosy cheeks and azure eyes and a smile that would have made everything right with the world, had she lived to bestow it on her daughter on a daily basis.

Bee gazed at her mother's portrait for a moment until her father's words brought her back to herself.

"How are your lessons going so far?"

"Awful," Bee muttered. Lying to her father was occasionally unavoidable, but she tried to be as truthful as possible the rest of the time to make up for it. "It's been the worst week of my life."

Papa chuckled. "Do you not like Miss Hilton?"

"I… I don't *dislike* her," she said in an effort to be fair. "She's calm and patient, and she's not cruel."

"Then what seems to be the problem?"

"They want me to learn *everything*. I have about a dozen new subjects, I'm dreadful at all of them, and they're so boring! And Malorie keeps hinting that I'll be a disgrace when I come out

CHAPTER 4

if I don't master them all."

Papa listened patiently, his expression solemn. After a pause, he said, "I'm afraid this is my fault. I ought to have engaged a governess for you when you first began learning to read. But you were having such fun, and I wanted you to enjoy the freedom of being a child. I guess I lost track of things after your mother passed and didn't realize how fast you were growing. Can you forgive me, love?"

Bee had never seen such a remorseful, forlorn look on her father's face, and she wanted to erase it immediately. She rounded his desk and put her arms around him, resting her head on his shoulder. "Of course I do, Papa. It is only that beginning new things is so very difficult."

"It is," he agreed, "but you'll gain competence before you know it. What if, at the end of each week, you demonstrate for me what you've learned? I want to see your progress, and I promise to be suitably impressed."

Bee was relieved to see a glint of laughter in her father's eyes. "Yes, let's. Starting next week," she added. "I have nothing whatsoever to show you this week." She kissed his cheek, and he pulled her in for a tight hug.

***

By the time Winston rode up, Bee was already throwing punches at Harry's padded hand.

"We're sparring today," she called up to him.

"Says who?"

"Me and Harry."

"Harry and I," Winston corrected automatically.

Bee stuck her tongue out at him. "You sound like Miss

Hilton."

If anyone else had compared him to a governess, he would have planted him a facer. But Bee was Bee, and a girl, and her insults held no bite. Winston dismounted and retaliated by picking up a pinecone and lobbing it lightly at her. Bee yelped in surprise as the tiny missile made contact.

"Why are we sparring today?" He grinned.

"Because I've had the worst week." Bee scowled. "I've only started half of the subjects I'm supposed to learn, and I still desperately need to hit something."

Winston glanced at Harry, who winked. "Let's take a bit more anger out on the target, Miss Snow," the groom said. "You need to think straight when you're sparring, and we don't want to send Master Graham home bloodied."

Winston narrowed his eyes at the groom, but the truth was that Bee was a good fighter. She was smaller than he was, but she was ferocious.

She was out of breath by the time she was done hitting the target. Winston stood by with his hands in his pockets. He'd had some bad days of lessons, but never anything he'd had to work out with such violence.

"You ready?" she asked, grinning.

Winston knew he ought to tell her no. After the last black eye he'd given her, he'd promised himself not to raise a fist to her again. But that answer died long before it reached his tongue. He would do whatever she asked, just like always, because he lived to see that fierce grin aimed his direction. He wouldn't let the pressure she was under at home crush that fiery spirit.

With a single, sharp nod, he slipped on the padded practice gloves Harry handed to him and to Bee and took up his position across from her. As they faced off, light on their feet, Harry gave them another lesson on the science of fighting, on analyzing their opponent's defenses and judging how best to exploit their weaknesses, and on how to spot the signs of an incoming hit before the fist was swung. Bee swung at Winston a few times; he blocked her easily. He aimed a couple of halfhearted jabs toward her midsection; she dodged back and glared at him.

"Fight like you mean it, Winston."

"Can't." He frowned back. "Against you, I *don't* mean it."

Bianca threw up her hands and turned to Harry. "This is impossible. How am I supposed to learn to fight if he won't hit me?"

Chuckling, Harry declared it time to return home anyway. "And you *are* learning, Miss Snow. Your form is consistently improving, and half of the fight goes on in your head."

Bee leveled her glare back at Winston. "You'd better get over this chivalrous nonsense," she muttered. "This afternoon was the most fun I've had all week, and I won't let you ruin it."

Winston gaped at her. With one more good glare, she turned on her heel and stalked over to mount her horse, riding away without a backward glance. Winston mounted up and rode home slowly, fighting within himself. He couldn't bear to hurt Bee again, but it was miserable to have her angry with him.

***

Bee spent the next three weeks practicing scales on the pianoforte and memorizing French nouns. She didn't enjoy her lessons any more than she had the first few days, but she gradually found them moderately less overwhelming. Miss

Hilton was kind but relentless, unwilling to accept anything less than perfection before moving on. As the weeks stretched on, Bee grew accustomed to the new schedule and stricter expectations. Even the process of learning new things became easier.

On Friday afternoon, Bee spent a half hour in Papa's study, telling him what she could remember about William the Conqueror and discussing the tea tray in French. They both ended up laughing as she mixed up her words and called the cake a chair. Bee was still giggling as she turned toward her room to change into a riding habit.

"Bianca, dear," came Malorie's voice from the back parlor. Bee paused in the open doorway. Her stepmother was at the writing desk with papers and ink strewn across it. She looked up at Bee and smiled, but the smile didn't reach her eyes. "When you go out, will you please ask Mrs. Cole to come discuss the menu for tomorrow? Thank you."

Bee nodded and disappeared up the stairs. It was odd, that Malorie would ask her to run an errand like that, because the back parlor had a bell she could pull to summon a servant to do it. But Bee had already learned not to talk back to her stepmother, and she never minded an excuse to go to the kitchen. Her stomach rumbled at the thought.

She changed quickly and burst into the kitchen, startling the cook and the two kitchen maids.

"Good heavens, Miss Snow!" Mrs. Cole, a smallish woman with frizzing copper hair and perpetually flushed cheeks, pressed her hand to her heart. "Don't crash about like that! You're lucky none of us were holding knives to drop."

"Sorry," Bee said quickly. "Lady Eston wants to speak to you about tomorrow's menu. She's in the back parlor."

CHAPTER 4

Mrs. Cole wiped her hands on her apron and untied it, hanging it on a hook. "Very well. Run along now." She left the kitchen.

Bee looked from the kitchen maids to the tray of cooling blueberry scones on a table. She looked back at the maids, who were watching her with carefully straight faces. "You won't tell, will you?"

The younger one, probably no older than Bee, twitched her lips as she tried to control her grin. The older one merely nodded and looked back at the pastry she was braiding, enabling her to say later that she saw nothing amiss.

Bee grinned, grabbed a napkin, and tied up three scones in the cloth. Then she slipped out the scullery door and went to find Harry at the stable.

Winston was sitting against the trunk of a tree with a book when they rode up.

"What book?" Bee asked unceremoniously.

"Johannes Kepler." Winston closed the cover. "Mathematics, astronomy, magic... He seems to have written about all of it, and it is apparently impossible to succeed at university if I haven't already read it three times over, or so Mr. Turbot says." He stashed the book in the saddlebag that lay beside him. "What do you have there?"

"Scones." Bianca dismounted and settled on the ground beside her friend.

"Kitchen raiding again? I'd thought you had reformed."

"Why on earth would you think that?"

"You haven't nicked any treats since before Lady Eston arrived."

Bee thought back. "I've been preoccupied," she said finally. "And today it was too easy. I couldn't pass up such a fail-proof opportunity." She untied the napkin and laid it on her lap.

She spoke a familiar spell-word, and one of the scones lifted off the napkin and rose to head height. Bee leaned in and bit off a corner while her magic held it level. Beside her, Winston sat forward too. Without warning, he spoke a spell-word of his own. The floating scone flew toward him. He caught it out of the air and took a bite.

Bee's eyes widened. "Why haven't you taught me that one yet? Does the spell just call it to you, or can you send it anywhere?"

"Anywhere," Winston said, gulping down the bite he'd been chewing. "But you have to pay extra attention and be very aware of where you're aiming."

He levitated the second scone with one word and with another sent it soaring over to Harry beside the horses. The groom spluttered an oath that ought not be spoken around young ladies before taking the scone and saying, "Many thanks, Master Graham and Miss Snow."

Bee grinned. "Show me how." She levitated the third scone.

With one finger, Winston pushed it back to the napkin. "Eat first. We'll practice with a pinecone. It's not an easy spell, and your food will drag all over the ground before you get it right."

Bee took a bite of her scone and chewed, nodding. When they'd finished eating, they found a pinecone. Winston taught Bee the spell-word. It took several tries before he said she was pronouncing it right.

"What language is this, anyway?" she demanded, exasperated.

"Magic." Winston shrugged. "Spells are made by combining parts of different languages. The greater age and variety of languages, the stronger the spell. This one has Hebrew,

Sanskrit, and Greek."

Bee blinked at him. "I hope Miss Hilton doesn't decide I need to know all that."

Winston laughed. "She probably won't. You won't be studying it at university, after all."

She scowled at him and his unwelcome reminder that he was soon to be leaving for Oxford and that women couldn't study there.

Her opinions on the subject were no secret. Winston nudged her shoulder with his. "Do you really want more years of lessons?"

"No," Bee grumped. "But it'd be nice to have the option."

Winston nodded. "I agree. And I'll teach you anything you like."

"So you're definitely going to be studying magic, then?"

He nodded again. "My father believes that the law would set me up better for my duties as an earl, but can you picture me sitting through those lectures?" He made a face.

"All right, Mr. Magician. Finish teaching me this spell."

Chapter 5

A week before Winston was due to leave for Oxford, Papa invited the family from Pinehurst for dinner. It was a common occurrence, particularly during the winter, when the weather didn't allow for visiting friends farther away. But Bianca felt like this visit carried a weight, a significance, that none of the others had. This was the beginning of goodbye.

It was also different from other dinners because Malorie insisted that Bee dress up and use this event as practice for how to behave in company, rather than treating it as a family dinner as she normally would. She'd spent half an hour sitting still while a maid braided and pinned her hair into an elegant knot, and she'd donned the pink dress that Papa had brought home from town for her, suppressing a shudder as she did. It was her newest and nicest, and she appreciated her father's thoughtfulness. But must it be pink?

She'd only been waiting in the drawing room with Papa and Malorie for a few minutes before Lord and Lady Rowland were announced and ushered in. Winston followed his parents but froze at the threshold as his gaze found Bee. His jaw slackened, and he stared. Bee felt her cheeks grow hot, certain her face was now a much darker pink than the pastel shade of her dress.

CHAPTER 5

Of course Winston would be shocked to see her in this color that everyone knew she loathed. But she could bear it for an evening if her friend would stop gaping as if he'd never seen her in an evening gown before.

Winston's mother leaned close to him and murmured something, which snapped him out of his stupor. He responded with a soft sound of assent and stepped farther into the room, just as a footman appeared to announce dinner. The couples paired off to move to the dining room, leaving Winston to escort Bee.

"Not a word about my dress, if you please," she hissed at him as she took his arm.

"You mean I shouldn't point out that it's the color you swore at age six that you would never, *ever* wear again?"

Bee glared at him. "Yes, that's precisely the type of comment I'd hoped to avoid."

He grinned. "It's a shame you hate it, because you look…" He swallowed and shook his head. "It looks nice on you."

Bee rolled her eyes but said nothing as they entered the dining room and took their seats. She wanted to make some kind of scathing remark so that she wouldn't have to feel the effects of his simple but sincere compliment. She didn't want to feel pretty in this dress, in pale pink, of all colors.

After dinner, Bianca retired to the drawing room with Malorie and Lady Rowland while Winston stayed behind with their fathers. She doubted Winston would share in the port, but she didn't blame him for staying with the gentlemen rather than sitting with her through the social trifles of the ladies' conversation. It was all shallow gossip and fashion. Bee knew that Lady Rowland was capable of more meaningful conversations, but Malorie was still new, and it was probably easier for the ladies to connect over what they'd seen and heard in town. Of course, that left Bee out of the conversation entirely, which appeared to suit Malorie. Lady Rowland addressed her comments to the room at large and smiled at Bee to include her, but Malorie showed no such compunction. So Bee sat stiffly on a chair to the side, her hands knotted together in her lap, and she used all her concentration to keep a vapid smile on her face and to not clutch her knuckles so tightly they turned white.

Lord Rowland was the first to rejoin them, and Bee nearly glared a hole in the door as she waited for Winston to follow. What was taking him so long? A few minutes later, he entered behind her father. Papa gave him a clap on the shoulder as if to punctuate whatever they'd been discussing before joining the other parents.

Winston crossed the room to take the chair next to Bee.

"What were you and my father discussing for so long?" She leaned over to whisper, untangling her tight fingers and resting her hands on the arms of her chair. "You were gone for *ages*."

"It was less than five minutes."

"It *felt* like ages," she muttered.

"Good to know you missed me," he teased.

Bee was about to demand a real answer when Lady Rowland addressed a question to her, and once Bee had made her answer, Winston changed the subject.

***

For the next two weeks Bee endeavored, and almost managed, to forget that Winston was leaving. They met in the woods each afternoon as they had for years. They sparred whenever

CHAPTER 5

she could coax him to. They shared tea cakes that Bee swiped from the kitchen. But they carefully avoided mentioning university, magic, or Winston's impending absence. Of course, the pretense couldn't last forever, but it was still a blow to Bee when Winston addressed the issue.

"I won't be able to come tomorrow." He was sitting against the base of a tree, dusting biscuit crumbs from his hands. Bee sat on a low stump nearby, nibbling at her own pastry. Suddenly, it tasted like sand in her mouth. "Last-minute preparations, you know. I leave the next day."

Bee nodded dully. She glanced at him; he was studying his hands, avoiding her eyes.

"If you ever need me for anything, my mother can get a message to me." He flicked his gaze up to hers.

She let out a slightly forced laugh. "I must be hearing things. I could have sworn I heard the unimpeachable Winston Elliot Graham suggesting a clandestine correspondence."

"No," he muttered, his color rising. "But I'm serious, Bee. If you ever need anything—anything at all—Mother will get your message to me." His intense gaze held hers for a moment before she dropped her eyes to her uneaten half a biscuit.

"Thanks," she said softly.

"Actually, speaking of Mother, do you think you might visit her sometimes? She'll miss me, and it would be nice for her to have company."

Bee nodded, a lump forming in her throat. She swallowed it back. She wouldn't cry, not over something as mundane as growing up. That would only make leaving harder for Winston.

When she was sure her voice wouldn't tremble, she said, "I'll miss you too. And I'll be glad to visit Lady Rowland."

Winston nodded and got to his feet. "Remember to learn what they teach you so that I can show you around London."

She nodded.

"I guess… goodbye, then."

Bee stood, tossed the remains of her biscuit into the woods so an animal could enjoy what she wouldn't, and looked up at her friend. "Make sure you write to your mother more than twice a year," she demanded. If her only news of Winston would be through Lady Rowland, his letters had better not be scarce.

He smiled. "I'll do my best."

"Do better."

He laughed. "Bye, Honeybee."

He opened his arms for a hug, and she wrapped her arms around his waist, burying her face in his chest so that he couldn't see the tears that had risen at the private nickname. This goodbye felt so much more final than any of the times he'd gone to town for the spring. He'd be home at Christmas and between terms, but it wouldn't be the same. He wasn't a boy anymore, or not for much longer. Their childhood friendship would change, and she was afraid he'd outgrow her once he was surrounded by other young men like himself.

They stepped back awkwardly. Winston swung himself into the saddle, hesitated as if he wanted to say something, then shrugged, waved, and rode off. Bee watched him go. The jingling of tack behind her drew her attention to Harry and the horses.

"Shall we ride the long way around the park on the way back, Miss Snow?" His expression was compassionate, and Bee wondered for a second what her friendship with Winston looked like to him, having watched them together daily for years.

But a longer ride was exactly what she needed to get her emotions under control. "Thank you, Harry." She mounted and turned Diamond toward home.

Chapter 6

For the first week after Winston left, Bee avoided going to the woods. Their special spot wasn't the same without him. But riding along the familiar trails through the park wasn't exciting enough to counteract the boredom of the schoolroom. By the middle of the second week, Bee needed a change.

"We're riding to Pinehurst today," she informed Harry as they trotted out of the stable yard. "It's time I pay a call on Lady Rowland."

It was nice to have a destination again, and the ride to the neighboring estate went quickly. Harry took the horses to the stables to wait while the butler showed Bee into the house.

"Her ladyship is in the peony room," he informed her, leading her down a hall to a small parlor and knocking at the door to announce her.

When Bee entered the parlor, she could see how it had gotten its name. The furniture was all cream and pink and gold, and the walls were papered with large flowers that somehow looked sweet and elegant rather than gaudy. A small fire burned in the grate. Lady Rowland set aside her sewing and stood up, coming over to envelop Bee in a warm hug.

"I'm so glad you came, dear," Winston's mother said. "You'll take tea with me?" Without waiting for a response, she called for refreshments then led Bee back to the couch.

Bee had never noticed before just how much Winston resembled his mother. Her hair was a shade lighter gold, but her eyes were the same bright blue. Her warm smile made Bee miss Winston more than ever. She cleared her throat. "Winston said you might be lonely with him gone."

Lady Rowland patted Bee's hand. "It's just two of us rattling around this big old house now. I'm of half a mind to stay in town until Winston's term ends. The house is smaller, and there are always friends about, even out of season when entertainments are few."

Bee's heart sank at the idea of losing Winston's family as well. "I do hope you won't," she said earnestly. "I'll come visit every day if it means you'll stay."

"You're too sweet, dear." Lady Rowland beamed. "That's not necessary, though I wouldn't object to a visit or two a week." She picked up her sewing and began to work while she talked. "Now, tell me about your lessons. What is your governess teaching you?"

Bianca would have gladly spoken of anything but lessons, but she found Lady Rowland easy to talk to despite the subject. She expressed her distaste for drawing and discovered that Lady Rowland had never been much of an artist either.

"Music was a different story," Winston's mother said. "I've always loved music and dancing."

Bee made a face. "I can't say I love either, though I haven't learned many dances yet, and I still stumble through those I know."

"What about your magic lessons? Winston used to tell me about the spells he taught you."

Bee blushed that her secret lessons were not so secret at all. "They're fascinating, by far my favorite subject aside from geography. Were you as magically inclined as Winston is?"

Lady Rowland laughed and shook her head. "He did not get that gift from me. My brother was a passable magician, and one of my sisters did the best illusions, but my magic was as abysmal my drawing."

Bee couldn't help grinning.

"No, Winston has always had an affinity for it," his mother went on. "I'm glad to see him pursuing his passion at university."

They had a pleasant tea, then Bee excused herself to go home.

"Thank you again for coming, dear." Lady Rowland embraced her again, then held her at arm's length. "Will you come again next week? Can you be spared for a whole morning to sit with me, do you think?"

"I'll ask Miss Hilton. If I promise to work on embroidery while I'm here, she may let me."

Bee said *embroidery* as if it were a dirty word, and Lady Rowland laughed.

"I would be incredibly grateful for your sacrifice." She grinned with the same teasing humor as her son. Despite the pang of wistfulness for her absent friend, Bee grinned in return.

Bianca's request to Miss Hilton went almost exactly as predicted, so the following Wednesday saw her settled into the peony room across from Lady Rowland with her work bag and what was supposed to become a pillow. Nothing could have made the sewing enjoyable, but Lady Rowland's cheerful company made the time pass faster than Bee expected. Winston had sent his mother a short letter, just a few lines to

CHAPTER 6

say that he was settled in, his rooms were comfortable, and he'd had his first lessons. He wasn't at the top of his class, but he wasn't behind either, and he was optimistic for the term. Bee heard the news with an uncomfortable feeling in her gut, which she did her best to ignore.

Winston's mother invited her to come again the next week, and it soon became a settled thing: Wednesdays were the time for visiting and handiwork that Bee couldn't be induced to do at any other time. She enjoyed her calls at Pinehurst, but they certainly didn't ease the endless, jealous wondering about what kinds of fascinating things Winston was learning and doing at Oxford.

***

Bianca's lessons continued to increase in difficulty. She had made rapid progress in French, to her governess's astonishment, and was now embarking on Italian.

"I'll say this for you, Miss Snow," the older woman said. "You may not always enjoy what we're learning, but you learn it thoroughly. Once you memorize something, it's in your head for good."

Bee couldn't deny this, but she really only found it a valuable skill when it came to remembering spells. She never forgot spell-words once she'd mastered them, and all of her spells worked at least moderately well on the first or second try.

Miss Hilton deemed this a solid foundation to teach Bee more difficult spells, including her first illusion. Bee couldn't help noticing that the spell-words included fragments of more languages now. As Winston had predicted, Miss Hilton didn't teach Bee about the languages or how the spell-words were made up. She simply taught her the next word and explained in detail what image Bee should be concentrating on when she said it.

The first illusion was a small one: taking an empty teacup and making it appear full. Bee sat and stared at the empty cup for five full minutes, repeating the word at intervals, before a wet sort of shimmer filled the cup for a second before disappearing between one breath and another.

"Nearly there," Miss Hilton encouraged calmly from the other side of the table. "Focus on what you *want* to see, not on what your eyes are telling you."

By the end of that first lesson, the shimmer came more often and more quickly, but it refused to look any more like tea. It took a week of practice before the cup would fill with what appeared to be tea with milk and sugar, exactly the way Bee liked it. Of course, the first time she'd succeeded in filling the cup, she was so amazed that she dipped her finger in the liquid and the spell dissolved.

"In time you'll be able to expand the illusion to include the sensation of touch as well," Miss Hilton assured her. "You will be able to make it feel as wet and hot as real tea." She insisted that Bee practice the illusion every time she finished an actual cup of tea, refilling the cup with magic before allowing the servants to take the empty tea things away.

The next illusion was to grow a flower. As it was autumn, most of the garden had gone by, but there were still plenty of blooms in the hothouse. Bee was instructed to choose a flower and then to spend time studying it. She must examine its color, texture, and scent. She must get a feel for how the petals overlapped, how the stem attached, how the head nodded in the breeze. That last was a bit tricky in the hothouse, but that

CHAPTER 6

didn't faze Miss Hilton. Bee was to get to know the flower so well that she could see it in her sleep.

It was an odd assignment, Bee thought, but she didn't mind. She'd always loved spending time in the pleasure gardens while Papa was away, and she rarely explored the hothouses. There were so many bright flowers to choose from, but Bee finally settled on a tulip: deep wine red and silky soft. Sitting still wasn't her greatest strength, but by the end of a half hour, that tulip was indelibly imprinted on her mind.

When they returned to the schoolroom, Miss Hilton placed a long blade of meadow grass in a tumbler on the table and instructed Bee to make the grass look like her tulip. She taught Bee the spell-word and sat back to watch as Bee frowned at the grass.

After a few minutes of nothing happening, Miss Hilton said, "Try closing your eyes. You might visualize it more easily."

Bee obeyed. She spoke the word and held the image of the tulip in her mind, imagining it plucked from its pot and sitting in the tumbler before her. She heard Miss Hilton shift slightly in her seat, and very carefully, without letting go of the tulip picture, she opened her eyes.

The tulip leaned against the side of the tumbler, its head bobbing gently. Bee gasped. Instantly, the grass was grass again.

"Well done, Miss Snow." Miss Hilton was smiling. "We will keep practicing this spell until nothing can break your focus."

"Yes, ma'am," Bee whispered, still staring at the tumbler in awe.

***

Bee's life fell into a comfortable rhythm for the next few months, with lessons, visits to Pinehurst, horseback rides, an occasional stolen pastry, and accomplishment demonstrations for Papa every week. Malorie never requested special demonstrations for herself, but she occasionally stopped into the schoolroom to observe. She nodded approval at Bee's French but pressed her lips together in disapproval at the weak Italian.

"How are you not making better progress with this, Bianca, dear?" she asked. "It's a Romance language just like French. They have the same basis in Latin."

Bee opened her mouth to protest, but Malorie interrupted before she could say anything, requesting to see the latest illusion.

Bianca took a deep breath and looked to Miss Hilton. The governess's expression was blank and closed off, and Bee wondered if the woman was as little fond of Malorie as she was herself.

"Go ahead, Miss Snow. We're due for your magic lesson now anyway."

Bee levitated the vase full of wilting meadow grass she was currently using and floated it to the table in front of her. Then she closed her eyes and began the illusion spell. She'd mastered one tulip; now she was trying to build a bouquet. So far she could hold three flowers in her head at once, and she was working on adding a fourth. When she opened her eyes, she could see the three tulips and a fourth flickering in and out of sight. The illusion faded. Bee glanced up at her stepmother.

Malorie raised her eyebrows and huffed, "Hm," before giving Miss Hilton a curt nod and leaving the room.

"What did she mean by that?" Bee muttered as she scowled at the door.

CHAPTER 6

"You're making excellent progress," the governess said. "My lady is not an educator."

That was all Miss Hilton would say on the matter.

***

In late November, Bianca awoke to a white world. Snow had begun to fall overnight, and it fell still—fat, heavy flakes that swirled and gusted and made it impossible to see the orchard wall out her window. Bee's heart sank. There was no way she could ride to Pinehurst in this, and the snow was deep enough that no carriage could make the trip either. She sighed and dejectedly picked at her breakfast. She'd miss her weekly break from lessons, and she was sure that the week she couldn't visit would be the one that Lady Rowland received a new letter from Winston.

That night the snow changed, mixing with rain and sleet to pound sideways against the windows. The glass rattled in the wind, and Bee couldn't sleep. She dozed fitfully, the storm noises a constant refrain in her dreams. The weather had not abated by the time she woke up. The snow on the ground had subsided into a thick gray slush, and by the following morning, the slush had frozen into solid ice.

Bee plodded through her lessons, having spent another sleepless night listening to the wind and freezing rain. When Malorie stopped in to observe for a half hour, Bee was too tired to care what criticisms she'd receive. She yawned hugely, trying to stifle it with her hand, but there was no hiding it.

Malorie raised an eyebrow. "You look dreadful, Bianca. I think it's time we learned some new spells."

Bee blinked at her, feeling stupid. Why would weariness

require spells? And Malorie never taught her magic. She glanced at Miss Hilton, but the governess busied herself with sheet music at the spinet and left the viscountess to her impromptu lesson.

"When you have your Season, you must always look your best. The *haute ton* is constantly watching with sharp eyes, and gossip abounds. You must give them no ammunition. Do you understand?"

"Yes, my lady," Bee said, though she felt like she was missing an important connection.

"There will be nights when you return from a ball exceedingly late, and it doesn't do to have bags under your eyes in the morning. You're too young to paint your face, so you need a glamour spell."

She then taught Bee the spell-word, instructing her to sit at her vanity and hold the hand mirror. "You must hold in your mind, very clearly, the effect you wish to create as you speak the spell. Once it's done, you can relax your attention and the glamour will hold for several hours." Malorie put her hand on the mirror and guided it upward so that Bee could see herself in the glass. "Now. Erase those shadows under your eyes."

Bee imagined herself looking fresh and awake, her skin bright and not shadowed or sagging. She spoke the spell-word, and her image in the mirror shifted. It was as if she'd had a full night's restful sleep between one breath and the next.

"Wow," she whispered.

Malorie's mouth curved upward in the smirk that served her for a smile when she was with Bianca. "There are more spells like that to learn, but we'll stop with the one for today. Continue, Miss Hilton," she directed the governess, who had been watching nearby, before sailing out of the schoolroom.

CHAPTER 6

Bee's lessons continued, but she was now distracted for a whole new reason. She couldn't stop thinking of this new spell's potential. She'd never have to lie about a riding accident to cover for a fighting injury again. Bee couldn't wait to share the spell with Winston, but then she remembered with a pang that he was at Oxford, and she wouldn't see him until Christmas.

Chapter 7

A few weeks later, less than a fortnight before Winston was to return home for the Christmas holidays, Bee started to cough. At first it was merely a mild annoyance, and as it led Miss Hilton to postpone her singing lesson, Bee didn't mind it. The cough was marginally worse the next day, but still nothing to worry about. Bee drank her tea with honey instead of milk and sugar and went about her lessons.

That night she woke up shivering and sweating, and she called weakly for Miss Hilton to ring the bell to have her fire made up again. She would have rung it herself, but her whole body ached with the chills, and she couldn't get herself out of bed. When the governess entered the room, she took one look at Bee and hurried over, laying a cool hand on her forehead.

"You're burning up, child," she said softly. "Get some rest. I'll be back in a moment."

Bee nodded, though she didn't feel like she was burning, unless icicles burned. She shivered under the covers until Miss Hilton returned in her dressing gown and slippers with a housemaid in tow. The maid built up the fire. Bee didn't feel the heat, but she fell into a restless doze before she could ask for more blankets.

CHAPTER 7

Bianca lost track of time. Night passed and the following day. Papa visited hourly. Miss Hilton remained by her side, coaxing her to have some tea or lemonade or barley water. Bee only managed a few swallows of whatever she was given. She ached, and she shivered, and she kicked her blankets off only to pull them back up to her chin a moment later.

And through it all, she coughed.

She couldn't take a full breath without a spasm of coughing overtaking her. Her body was wracked with them, and she lay exhausted and weak each time one passed. She passed in and out of fitful sleep, unaware of the worried looks the adults were giving each other.

***

Winston's heart was in his throat as he took the letter from the express courier. What could have happened that would require his mother to send an express when she knew from his last letter that he'd be riding home from Oxford tomorrow?

He tore the paper in his haste to break the seal, and his eyes darted over the words. Short and to the point, which his mother's letters never were, the message explained that Miss Bianca Snow had come down with winter fever, and everyone was overcome with worry.

"The doctor's been to see her every day and has given them medicine for her," his mother wrote, "but Mr. Winchell is at the other end of his circuit and won't be here for weeks, if he even has a spell that could help." Mr. Winchell was the nearest country magician. He was a decent enough fellow, and a capable magician, but he was spread too thin as the only magician serving their part of the country. And medical spells that actually worked were rare.

Winston had just finished his last exam this morning, and he'd intended to spend the afternoon packing and purchasing a few final gifts for his parents, but instead he jogged to the Bodleian Library, dodging the bustle of students celebrating the end of term. The library was sure to have some spells that would help Bee.

Hours later, with the help of an impressively patient and knowledgeable librarian, Winston left the building into the gathering dusk. He had only two new spells to show for all that time spent searching, but they were from reputable sources and reported to be effective. Now that he had spells that could ease Bee's discomfort and promote healing, he couldn't bear to be away from her another minute.

He threw some clothing haphazardly into a bag, remembering at the last minute to tuck the gifts he'd purchased into the bag as well. He sent a message to the stables to have Grayling readied, then stuffed a hunk of bread leftover from breakfast into his pocket. Winston gulped down some cold, bitter coffee to keep himself alert through his nighttime ride, though he doubted he'd need it. His worry over Bee would keep him going.

The middle of the night had passed by the time he rode up to Eston Hall's entrance. Winston's conscience twinged at the rudeness of waking up the household at this time of night, but he couldn't wait. Bee needed these spells. The two families had been friends long enough that propriety could be set aside this once. He tied Grayling's reins to a post and pounded on the door until the flustered butler appeared.

"Master Graham! Do you know what time it is, sir?"

"Near enough. I need to see Bianca and Miss Hilton

immediately."

"At three o'clock in the morning?"

A voice from behind the butler said, "What on earth is it, Hawke?"

"Lord Eston!" exclaimed Winston, hoping that Bee's father would listen. "I have a spell to lower Bee's fever."

"Graham? That you, son? Come in! Hawke, don't leave him standing on the step like that."

The butler stepped back and allowed Winston inside. Lord Eston, always polished and genteel, looked pale and drawn as he tied his dressing gown at his waist. Winston stopped in front of him and bowed, aware of how disheveled he must look himself from riding hard all night.

"I'd never have woken you if it weren't so urgent, my lord."

"It's a spell for Bee, you said? Go right up." Eston nodded to a footman, who appeared at his elbow and gestured for Winston to follow him upstairs. "See me in the library when you're done."

Winston ascended the stairs after the footman, who lightly tapped on a door partway down the hall. A rustle of footsteps then a small woman with gray hair coming loose from the knot at her neck and a slightly panicked look opened the door and shushed them.

"She's asleep, finally. What is it?"

"Miss Hilton?" Winston whispered. "I'm Winston Graham. I have spells that should help Bee."

A cough sounded from deeper within the room, and the woman glanced over her shoulder. She opened the door and waved him in. "Come on, then."

She turned and led the way into the sickroom. Winston followed. The sight of Bee squirming restlessly under the covers sank his heart into his stomach. Her breathing was shallow. A sheen of sweat coated her gray-tinged skin. Her dark hair had come loose from its braid and was plastered to her temples.

Winston swallowed hard. He'd known she was ill, but seeing it gutted him afresh. He fished in his pocket for the scrap of paper he'd written the instructions on. "I have two spells—for her cough and for her fever. The spell for the cough works best if you touch her skin, the closer to her lungs the better. I… er… would it be acceptable for me to touch her shoulder, just to demonstrate the spell so you can do it in future?"

Miss Hilton gave him a sharp look, but she nodded.

Winston took a deep breath and stepped forward, reading the spell-word again to ensure he had it perfectly right before casting it on his dearest friend.

Bianca's nightgown had shifted as she thrashed, sliding half off her left shoulder. Winston gently rested the tips of his fingers on her clammy skin, nearly gasping at the heat of her fever. He spoke the spell-word and stepped back. He wished he could press a kiss to Bee's forehead, but Miss Hilton's gaze bored into him. Both of them fixed their attention on the girl in the bed. After a moment, she took a deeper breath than she had since Winston had arrived, and she sighed.

Miss Hilton let out the breath she'd been holding in an unladylike whoosh. "Heavens above," she murmured. "Thank you, Master Graham."

"My pleasure," he said, forcing his gaze away from Bee's face. He had another spell to cast.

He reviewed the word for the fever spell, and this time he brushed sweaty strands of Bee's hair from her face before resting his palm gently on her forehead. He spoke the spell-word, then he withdrew his hand and stood breathless, watching and waiting. Miss Hilton perched on the edge of the chair beside the bed. After a few heartrending ticks of the clock in the schoolroom, Bianca's movements eased. She settled into her pillow, and soon the trembling, which Winston now realized was shivering from the fever, ceased as well. Miss Hilton dipped a cloth in cool water and laid it over Bee's forehead, brushing tentative fingers against her face.

"She's cooler," Miss Hilton said softly. She looked up at Winston, relief causing her eyes to glisten. "Thank you."

Winston nodded, unable to speak. He looked down at the paper in his hand. He slipped from Bianca's chamber and located paper and a pencil in the next room, copying out the two spells before returning to Bee's bedside. His hand shook as he handed it to Miss Hilton.

She pocketed it, saying, "Thank you again, Master Graham."

Winston bowed, cast one last look at Bee, who now seemed to be resting comfortably, and left the room. Lord Eston waited in the library, staring absently into the freshly built fire. Winston cleared his throat.

"Her fever's down." His voice was trembling just like the rest of him.

Eston turned. "How is she?" He sounded half choked, and Winston decided that no one would sound quite like themselves tonight.

"Resting. Her cough is eased for now, too."

Eston released a sigh. He nodded. "Thank you, son. You've done us a service that we won't soon forget."

"I did what I could, my lord," Winston said. He wouldn't forget today either. "If I could suggest, though…" Winston hesitated, knowing it wasn't his place to advise the running of another man's home. But it was for Bee's good, so he continued. "Miss Hilton will need to get regular sleep if she's to keep up the spells. Otherwise, she'll be at greater risk of catching the fever too."

"Mrs. Portman has been taking a shift with Bianca each night, and I've been sitting with her for a portion of the morning. Lady Eston might be in the family way, so we're keeping her from the sickroom. We'll make sure Miss Hilton rests."

"May I call again tomorrow?" Winston asked. "I could refresh the spells to spare Miss Hilton one casting at least."

"You're welcome to call anytime, Graham, after what you've done for us, and if you've a mind to cast more spells, I give you my leave to do so."

Winston bowed and left, riding Grayling slowly home to Pinehurst, where he startled all their own servants by arriving so early and unexpectedly. He was too tired to be sorry, however. Now that he'd gotten the spells to Bee, the anxiety that had kept him going all night drained from him. Bee wasn't out of danger yet; winter fever could last for weeks, and some never recovered. But she was young and strong, fierce and relentless. If anyone could hold onto life, she could. But that wouldn't stop him from visiting her every day while he was home, as soon as he'd gotten a few hours' sleep.

Chapter 8

Bee did a lot of sleeping.

The first few days she'd spent in bed had been a blur of torment. She remembered hearing snatches of voices: Papa, Miss Hilton, Mrs. Portman, another man who must have been the doctor. Then she had a vague idea that Winston had said something—though that must have been her illness-addled imagination, for what would Winston be doing *here*?—and she'd started to feel better. The coughing that had wracked her body in the beginning didn't hit her so often, and the aches and chills faded. But she was still excruciatingly tired. So she slept, and she woke to drink a little weak tea or lemonade, and then she slept some more. Miss Hilton was seated in the chair beside the bed most often when she woke, but sometimes it was the housekeeper. Once or twice, it was Papa.

Bee didn't know how much time passed this way. Gradually, she stayed awake a little longer each time, long enough to swallow some gruel that she'd never have stomached when she was healthy. Her mind registered it as invalid food, but she had no strength to protest. She fell back asleep.

Once when she woke up, Winston was there. He stood in the doorway, as if he'd just arrived. Maybe hearing him greet Miss

Hilton had been what had woken Bee. She blinked up at him, and he gave her a lopsided grin that dripped with concern.

"Morning, Honeybee."

She blinked slowly, stunned to see him there.

"How are you feeling?" he asked, reaching for the second chair that had been tucked into a corner and tugging it near the bed. He laid a paper-wrapped parcel beside her on the bed. "Merry Christmas."

"Christmas? Already?"

"Yesterday," Winston said. "Open it."

Bianca handed her cup back to her governess and picked up the parcel. She tugged on the ribbon and let the paper fall away to reveal a book—a beautiful, leather-bound copy of *The Arabian Nights' Entertainment*.

"Have you read them?"

Bee shook her head, gently turning the pages. Nurse had taught her to read using fairy tales and fables, but after that she'd read more histories and biographies than folk tales. She'd forgotten how much she liked them, and this collection was set in a faraway land—her favorite. Bee wanted to start reading right away, but she was already tired from holding her head up so long.

"Will you read to me?" She held the book out to her friend.

Winston exchanged a glance with Miss Hilton. "For a few minutes," he said. "And only if you eat something."

Bee sighed and let her head flop back. "Not gruel. Please." She caught the beginning of a smile from Miss Hilton. "Could I have toast with marmalade?"

"I'll send for some from the kitchen." Miss Hilton rose from her chair. "You may begin reading, Master Graham."

Winston opened the book and began reading about the

sultan, Shahryar, and his new bride, Scheherazade. Bee lay back and listened. Winston was a good reader. His voice was calm and soothing, and she easily lost herself in the story. Even so, her eyes were getting heavy long before Miss Hilton returned. Winston paused, and Bee looked up to see him watching her.

"I'm afraid I must stop for now," he said, placing the wrapping ribbon between the pages and closing the book. "If I read more, you'll fall asleep and fail to keep your end of the bargain."

"Never," Bee said, then had to cover a yawn. She laughed weakly. Though she wasn't coughing as much, her chest still felt tight, and deep breaths were difficult. A moment later, the governess arrived with the tray.

Winston rose and moved his chair back against the wall. "I'll leave you to keep your promise," he said with a bow and a wink at Bee. "I'll call again soon."

"Thank you," Bee said softly. She meant for the gift but also for coming, for being her friend, for making this day a little less tiresome.

Winston flashed her a quick smile and then disappeared through the door.

He came to visit again the next day. Bee was still sleeping a great deal, but she was staying awake longer, and Miss Hilton had been able to stop using the fever-reducing spell altogether. When she saw her friend in the doorway, Bee grinned.

"Look at me! I'm almost sitting!" She leaned back against the mountain of pillows that propped her up and raised her hands in mock victory. She'd been growing more and more exasperated with her condition, wishing to be back to her usual pursuits instead of confined to bed. Joking about it was the only way to cope without going mad.

Bianca could see that Winston, like Miss Hilton and Papa, took every small bit of improvement seriously. But he gamely pressed a hand to his heart and, with a grin, said, "I'm beyond honored to witness such a momentous occasion."

"You should be," she agreed. "We practically had an entire ceremony this morning, with maids bringing in pillows and Mrs. Portman fluffing them all so that they'd be exactly perfect. It may as well have been a parade, minus the brass band." Bee glanced at Mrs. Portman, who was knitting in her chair by the bed, but the housekeeper merely smiled.

Winston chuckled, as she'd hoped, and pulled over a chair. "Aside from victorious, how are you feeling?"

"Bored. There are only so many Italian conjugations I can review before I want to scream."

"Are you back to lessons already?" Winston looked taken aback.

"No, but I made the mistake of complaining of boredom to Miss Hilton this morning. My other lessons are too demanding, but she thought that reviewing languages might keep me occupied for a while."

"Did it help?"

Bee gave him a look. He ought to know by now what a stupid question that was. "It compounded the problem. I did learn *something*, however." She assumed a virtuous expression for a moment, before relaxing into a smile. "I've learned that being bored from having nothing to do is infinitely preferable to boredom by scholarly enterprise."

"How enlightening."

"Isn't it? But now you're here, and I'm making it your official responsibility to entertain me. Show me some magic I haven't seen. Read to me. Convince Mrs. Cole to send me up some

CHAPTER 8

cake." She waved a languid hand. "Use your imagination. I'm easily amused at this point."

Winston turned to Mrs. Portman. "Do you think Mrs. Cole would send her cake?"

The housekeeper shook her head. "Toast and jam is the sweetest thing she's sent up so far."

"What about scones? Muffins? Surely those aren't too sweet."

"You're too moderate by half," Bianca grumped. "I want cake."

Winston laughed. "But isn't a muffin better than nothing?"

Bee sighed. "I suppose. Mrs. Portman, may I please have some tea? And muffins or scones or whatever non-cake pastry I'm allowed that is more interesting than toast?"

Mrs. Portman set aside her knitting and got to her feet. "I'll bring something up, and I'll send in Miss Hilton to sit with you again. Shall I tell her you'd like to review mathematics this afternoon?"

Bee gasped, which turned into a cough. When she'd got herself under control, she scowled at the housekeeper. "You wouldn't."

"No, Miss Snow, I wouldn't, and I apologize for teasing. I'll bring up your tea in a moment."

When she'd left, Bee gave Winston a sly look. "Do you think she'll feel guilty enough for making me cough that she'll bring me a biscuit or a tart?"

He shook his head. "You have the sweetest sweet tooth of anyone I've met, Honeybee."

Bee rolled her eyes. "You would too if you'd had nothing but gruel and toast for days." She sighed dramatically. "Tell me a story, Scheherazade."

Winston gave her a pained look. "I'll read to you—*if* you never call me Scheherazade again."

Bee fought back her grin and placed a hand almost solemnly over her heart. "I promise as faithfully as you swore at age eight to stop calling me Honeybee."

He hid his face behind the book, and Bianca stopped holding back her smile.

Winston was still reading when Miss Hilton arrived at the same time as the tea tray. He paused and greeted the governess politely. Bee was more interested in the contents of the tray. Cold meat and salad, and scones to spread with blackberry jam, but…

"No cream?"

Miss Hilton smiled and took the seat Mrs. Portman had vacated. "Cream is not invalid food, and you know by now how strongly Mrs. Cole feels about the subject."

Bee sighed. "At least it's blackberry jam." She picked at the plate Miss Hilton put together for her while Winston went back to reading.

When Winston came to visit the following day, Bee was alone in her room, propped up in bed with a book resting against her knees. She closed it with a snap when a footman announced him. "Thompson, please let Miss Hilton know that Winston is here and be so good as to ask Mrs. Cole to send up tea for our guest." The footman bowed and left.

Winston lowered himself into the chair nearest the bed. "You just ordered tea, but you look like a cat who's caught a mouse. What's up?"

"I've figured out how to get cake." Bee smirked. "Mrs. Cole has a soft spot for you, I've heard, and she'd never force you to eat invalid food."

CHAPTER 8

"How could she have a soft spot? I've only met her once or twice, and that was years ago."

"Oh, it's not just her. They all do. You're the hero of Eston Hall." She fixed him with a sharp look. "Why didn't you tell me you brought those spells Miss Hilton has been using?"

Winston shrugged. "You'd have done the same for me."

"Doesn't mean I'm not grateful. Or that you'll get out of teaching the spells to me once I'm allowed to do magic again."

"Miss Hilton still won't let you do spells?"

Bee shook her head. "She says I'm too weak." She sighed. "She's right. I tried to go pick out another book to read, but I was out of breath before I reached the bookshelf." And the shelf in question was only on the other side of the schoolroom.

Bianca could see Winston's concern, but he seemed to know that she was tired of people fussing, because he only waved at the book she'd set aside and asked, "What are you reading then?"

Sermons for Young Ladies." She grimaced. "Mr. Fordyce is a complete bore, and I've a feeling he wouldn't like me much. But Miss Hilton has decided that I'm not too weak to pick up *some* of my lessons again." She shot the book an irritable glare. "I do wish this wasn't one of them. I suspect," she leaned closer and lowered her voice, "Malorie has been voicing her concerns over how far behind I'm falling."

"Has she said anything to you?"

Bee shook her head. "I haven't seen her since I fell ill. They said she's... you know..." She blushed and looked away. It was strange—she'd always been able to talk to Winston about anything, but she couldn't quite bring herself to mention human reproduction in front of an eighteen-year-old boy. "And she couldn't be exposed to the fever."

"It's lucky that you have Miss Hilton to look after you then," Winston said, just as Miss Hilton joined them.

"Very lucky," Bee agreed, with a bright smile for her governess.

A maid arrived with the tea tray, and Bee let out a hastily stifled squeal of delight when she saw what was on it. She cast a quick look at Miss Hilton and pressed her lips together to try to control her glee, but it was impossible. For the first time in ages, there was a plate of tea cakes on the tray. Bee sat up and put two on a plate for herself as Miss Hilton poured tea. She ate the first one in two bites, closing her eyes in ecstasy so that she couldn't see her governess's disapproving frown. When she'd swallowed, she met Winston's twinkling eyes with a grin.

"I now have double the reasons to call you a hero." She reached for another cake.

Winston chuckled. "I'm always happy to oblige. Though, you know, my service is only seen as heroic because you're so loved. You're the sweetheart of both our houses, remember—everyone would be devastated if anything happened to you."

Miss Hilton raised an eyebrow and handed Winston his cup. "I'll thank you, Master Graham, not to administer to her vanity any further." But there was a softness at the corners of her mouth that suggested she was hiding a smile, and she said nothing to disagree with his actual statement.

"Forgive me." Winston sketched a tiny bow from his seat, which Bee hadn't seen him do before. She wondered for a second if he'd been taught a hundred ways to bow in the same manner that she was being taught all the variations on the curtsy. "I hadn't been under the impression that Bee had much for vanity, but I beg your pardon for speaking indiscreetly."

CHAPTER 8

But his eyes flashed with suppressed laughter at Bee.

Chapter 9

All too soon, Winston had to return to Oxford for the start of the next term. Without his visits to look forward to, it was a matter of days before Bianca was thoroughly sick of seeing the walls of her own room. She pestered and begged and cajoled by turns until poor Mrs. Portman threw up her hands in exasperation.

"What would you have me do, Miss Snow? You can't walk to the drawing room. Shall I have your father come up to carry you down?"

"No, of course not. I'm not an infant to be carried everywhere." Bee had stood on her own two feet to wash and dress each morning, albeit with help, and by now she'd taken brief sojourns into the schoolroom and back. "I'm sure I can walk."

Without waiting for the housekeeper's consent, Bee swung her legs over the side of the bed and got up. She walked slowly but steadily from the bedchamber, through the schoolroom, and into the hall. She realized as she went that her feet were still bare on the cold wood floor, but she wasn't about to turn back now. At the top of the stairs, she discovered that she'd overestimated her recovery. Bee paused and leaned against the wall, out of breath. Mrs. Portman bustled up behind her.

"You see, Miss Snow? Now you've gone too far, and we must

get you back to bed before you have a relapse."

"Don't fuss, Mrs. Portman. I'd rather sit here in the hall for a while than go back to my room." She frowned. "There must be somewhere else I can go that's closer than the drawing room." It had been some time since she'd spent rainy days exploring the house and shadowing the housekeeper. "What about that parlor…?"

"The sunflower room, do you mean?" Mrs. Portman crossed the hall and opened a door. Light spilled through a window inside and lit the goldenrod upholstery, making the room glow like paradise. Bee walked to the doorway and looked in. The room was as clean as Mrs. Portman insisted everything be in Eston Hall, but it was obvious no one ever used this tiny parlor. There was a chaise longue across from the small fireplace, two chairs, and a low table, but that was all that fit. A large painting of sunflowers hung over the mantle, and the upholstery and drapes were bright yellow to match. It ought to have been a hideous room, but it somehow managed to feel cozy and happy. Bee liked it immediately.

"This was your mother's favorite sitting room," Mrs. Portman said softly, standing beside Bee with her hand still on the door.

"Does Malorie…?"

"Lady Eston prefers the back parlor downstairs."

Bee felt her heart lighten as she looked at the room. "I will take tea here today, I think." She crossed the few steps to the chaise and settled herself on it, relaxing back against the cushions. "And every day hereafter."

***

It was the middle of January by the time Bianca remembered that she'd missed Christmas. She'd procrastinated buying anything for Winston, though she'd purchased gifts for Papa and Malorie in the village shop. And then she'd been sick and he'd practically saved her life, and she hadn't given him anything. She was determined to make up for that.

After the initial danger, Lady Rowland had begun calling at Eston Hall every couple of weeks, spending time with Malorie in the parlor downstairs before joining Bee in the sunflower room for a few minutes before taking her leave. When she came at the end of January, she handed Bee a small but heavy object wrapped in brown paper and tied with a golden bow. Bee unwrapped the paper to see a jar filled with tiny golden sweets. Each had been molded into a small circle with the imprint of a bumblebee on top. "Winston wrote that he found this honey candy at a shop near the university and thought of you. Something about how you haven't been fed enough cake?"

"Honeybee," Bee laughed, though the sound came out somewhat choked by the lump in her throat. "He likes to tease me about my sweet tooth."

She bent to tuck the jar into her workbag, rummaging through it for a moment to compose herself. Bee straightened with a small book in her hand. "I was actually hoping you'd be able to pass this along for me, too, since I didn't have it ready for Christmas." She held the tiny book out to the countess. "Winston always writes down new spells as he learns them, and I thought he might like a book he could keep in his pocket."

She'd cut the paper and sewn the sheets together by hand, covering it with a scrap of deep blue silk. It was a small thing, the most she could manage in her weakened state, but she was proud of it.

Lady Rowland smiled and took the gift. "I'll send it with my next letter."

***

Malorie lost the baby.

She'd done everything right. She'd rested, she'd avoided the sickroom, she'd eaten when her churning stomach would allow it. But she'd only missed two months of bleeding before it came again, proving that the baby was gone.

Malorie sat before the hearth in her chamber, hugging a brocade pillow tightly to her, as if squeezing the pillow would help her hold back the tears. Weeping was terrible for the complexion. It aged one more than nearly anything else. And Malorie must maintain her good looks. In the absence of an heir, her beauty was all she had. If she couldn't produce a child, the least she could do was remain Lord Eston's lovely young wife, a pretty ornament on his arm when they went to town.

It was awful, all of it. Nothing about married life was the way she'd hoped. Nearly eight months of trying for a child, and the first time she'd had hope... nothing.

She could barely face the idea of going to town for the season. After such a disappointment, the best place to lick one's wounds was in private, away from the gossip and rumors and the constant need to put on a perfect façade. But she couldn't bear to stay in Eston Hall. It was bad enough that this was where she'd lost the baby. Worse still, she was daily subjected to talk of Bianca's improvement. Not that she wished ill on the girl—she hadn't wanted her to *die* of the fever—but must every single servant in the house talk of Miss Snow? Couldn't any of them see that she herself was suffering, and that they were adding salt to the wound?

Because Bianca Snow was living, breathing proof that Lord Eston's first wife had *not* failed to produce a child.

Malorie began to count down the days until they could go to town and leave Bianca and the painful memories of winter behind them.

***

By the time her parents left for town in March, Bianca was back to nearly her full complement of lessons. Miss Hilton eased her back into them, insisting that they break in the middle of the day for Bee to take a nap.

On warmer days, Bee was finally allowed out of the house for a short walk in the gardens. She was bundled in shawls and scarves and sat often on benches in the sun to keep from getting too out of breath.

"This is ridiculous," she groused to Harry one day when she'd walked to the stable to visit Diamond. She'd received a hard denial to her request to go for a ride. "I'll never get stronger if they don't let me push myself a little."

"If you push too hard, you'll get sick again, and then where would you be?"

Bee sighed. "You're supposed to take my side."

"Am I?"

She stuck her tongue out at his back when he turned away to get a curry brush, but she didn't argue when it was time to return to the house.

It was another two weeks before she was allowed to ride Diamond again with Harry at her side. They walked the horses

CHAPTER 9

slowly on easy trails within the park. When they dismounted in the stable yard, Harry took the reins from her and said gruffly, "Glad you're back, Miss Snow. Diamond missed you."

She could see the concern and affection he was trying to hide, and she grinned at him. "I'm counting on you to help me return to full strength," she said quietly. "I intend to ride as often as I can until I'm back to my old habits."

His eyes crinkled in a smile. "I'd expect no less, Miss Snow. You've a stronger spirit than any lass I've known."

It was another three weeks before Bee rode to the hideout in the woods. Harry had a big bundle tied to the back of his saddle. It was covered in a blanket, which he shook out and laid on the ground for her.

"You rest a bit while I get this set up," he said.

Bee sat on the blanket, watching him curiously. The bundle turned out to be a kind of scarecrow stuffed with straw and ashes. Harry bound it upright at chest height against a sapling with no low branches to get in the way.

"Is that…"

"A new target to practice on." Harry nodded. "You've been sick a long while, and you've lost muscle tone, so you'll throw punches at this to build up your strength and stamina again."

Bee got to her feet and rushed to give the groom a hug. Embracing a servant wasn't proper, but there was no one around to see. "That is one of the best gifts I've ever gotten."

Harry cleared his throat and stepped back. "Not a gift, miss, just a training tool." But his ears were red, and he looked pleased.

Bianca practiced with the scarecrow every day, at first only managing a few minutes before she was gasping for breath. She kept at it, imagining Winston returning from Oxford and seeing her hard at work. She grinned. He'd probably fall out of his saddle in alarm. But she was determined that by the time he came home before the summer term, she'd be strong enough to spar again.

Miss Hilton was pleased with Bee's recovery. She encouraged the daily afternoon rides, believing them—more or less correctly—to be responsible for her rapid improvement. As Bee's lungs were no longer troubled, the governess decided to add the final lesson back in: dancing. Bianca had no interest in crowded balls or dancing with strangers, but she could admit to herself that dancing had given her a bit more lightness of foot, which benefited her pugilistic tendencies, and it could help her rebuild her strength and stamina. She did her best to remember the steps as she pranced through the schoolroom with Miss Hilton for a partner, the only music being whatever the governess decided to hum.

***

When Papa and Malorie returned from town in late May, Bee was almost back to her old self. She was in a good mood now that Miss Hilton had finally decided that she was strong enough to practice magic again. Her mood faded quickly as Malorie proved to be just as critical as before, and her comments were sharper than ever. When her stepmother came to the schoolroom to judge the progress she'd made while they were gone, nothing seemed to please her. Bee knew her Italian was still atrocious, but she was also criticized for her singing—Malorie called her voice "warbly"—and her performance on the pianoforte—"I'm mystified how you can make such a lovely piece of music feel so expressionless, dear."

CHAPTER 9

Papa and Malorie had brought fabric home from town to have new dresses made for her in the current style. While the dressmaker was present, Malorie kept her comments to the cut and styling of the gowns, but when the dressmaker left, as she was dismissing Bee back to the schoolroom, she said, "I do hope you'll develop soon, dear. You have no figure to speak of, and it's not so very long before you'll have your come out."

Mortification made Bee's cheeks flush hotly, and she fled the room, glad that no one else had been there to hear it. She'd never much cared what she looked like, as long as her gowns were presentable, and she'd been proud of her muscles from boxing. But Malorie's words burrowed into her heart and made their home with the rest of the barbs her stepmother had spoken since she'd come to them.

Chapter 10

Bee didn't learn a single thing in her lessons that morning, and Miss Hilton chided her repeatedly for inattention. But Bee didn't care. She'd had a note from Lady Rowland: Winston was home. Only for a fortnight between terms, but after months without seeing him, she'd take whatever time she could get. She had too much pent up excitement to sit still, so when she was finally released from the schoolroom, she flew down to the stables. Winston might not get to the woods that early—for all she knew, he might not be able to come today at all—but if she had to wait, she could get Harry to give her another pugilism lesson. She was back to nearly full strength now, and he'd begun sparring lightly with her again.

There was no cause to worry. Harry had only just dismounted to take Diamond's head when the thud of hooves announced her friend's arrival. Bee slid out of the saddle and was already halfway to where Winston was dismounting before she got a good look at him.

She froze. This was not the same boy she'd said goodbye to in December. Was it? Had she missed the changes in him in her own illness-induced self-absorption? He was as tall as ever, maybe even a little taller, but he'd lost the gangly look that came from shooting up like a weed. He'd put on flesh and muscle, and his shoulders filled out his coat in a way they hadn't before. His dark blond hair had been cropped close. She missed the curls, but it suited him. It all suited him. She blinked, suddenly shy. In the past, when he'd been gone for weeks to town, she'd have hurled herself at him and hugged him tightly, but she couldn't possibly do that with this... man.

Winston, too, was frozen in place. His blue eyes, at least, were the same as ever, but he stared at her like a man dying of thirst beholding a glass of water, as if he could drink up the sight of her and quench his emptiness. Her mouth went dry and butterflies fluttered in her midsection.

"Hey, Bee," Winston said softly.

His familiar voice brought a burning to the back of her eyes, and she thought she might choke on all the unexpected emotions. She held out her hands to take his, and he grasped both of hers. Had his hands always been so much larger than hers? They enveloped hers completely and sent warmth up her arms.

Bee bit her lip. What was she supposed to do now? Her best friend had morphed into a gorgeous young man, and she was nervous around him as she'd never been before. She sought for something, anything, to bring the interaction back to familiar footing.

"Want to spar?" It was the only thing she could think of to break the awkward silence.

Winston frowned and shook his head. "I can't anymore, Bee. I should have stopped years ago. As a gentleman, I won't hit a woman, and there's no denying that you're a lady."

Bee's irritation flared, and she clung to the feeling because at least it wasn't new. She dropped his hands and stepped away.

"Am not. I haven't even come out yet."

Winston sighed. "I'm sorry."

Bee scowled and crossed her arms petulantly. She didn't want to be a lady. She didn't want to grow up. Everything needed to go back to the way it had been. Winston looked away. Silence stretched between them, threatening awkwardness and the ruin of their comfortable friendship.

He looked back at her after a minute, saying, "Mother wrote that you have a new spell to show me?"

It had been so long since she'd learned the glamour illusion that Bee had forgotten mentioning it to Lady Rowland during one of her visits. "I've only ever tried it with a mirror," she said, "but I'll see if it works without one."

She closed her eyes and visualized her appearance. Malorie had taught it to her as a way to hide flaws, but Bee had played with the spell when she was bored this spring, and she had mastered changing her eye color. Hair color was harder, because there was so much more of it. Now she chose one section of hair to imagine turning from black to a deep, rosy auburn. She murmured the spell-word, holding the image in her mind until she felt the spell take hold, then opened her eyes.

Winston was frowning at her pinned-up braids. "You can change your hair color?"

She shook her head. "So much more than that. It's a glamour illusion. I've managed to change my hair and eye color just for fun, but really it's for hiding things. I've seen Malorie use it to hide the lines at the corners of her eyes, and I've used it myself to appear less tired when I haven't slept well." She tilted her head and gave him a sly smile. "I thought it would be useful for covering bruises."

CHAPTER 10

He stared at her for a moment. "That's brilliant," he said finally. "Not that you'll have any more bruises to hide."

She waved the comment away. "Of course not. But just because you won't fight *me* doesn't mean you won't get into scraps with anyone else."

Winston nodded. "I got to town for a weekend this spring and had a go with Gentleman Jackson. Came away with quite the shiner."

"Your mother never said!"

"She didn't know. I went back to Oxford before she could see it." He smiled ruefully. "Care to teach me that spell?"

He pulled a pencil and the little book she'd made for him from his pocket and opened to a page near the end. As she told him the spell-word and how to perform it, she cast her eyes over his scribbled notes in the book. His writing was tiny, as if he were trying to squeeze as much into the pages as he could.

"Why are you writing so small?" She'd seen his penmanship before, on letters that his mother had shown her, and usually it was a large scrawl.

His ears grew red, and he muttered, "I didn't want to run out of space too soon."

"You goose!" Bee laughed. "I can make you another. I'll make you half a dozen if you like."

Winston smiled, and Bee again felt that odd fluttering in her stomach.

"How have your lessons been going?"

She shrugged. "Italian is impossible, and I still hate the pianoforte. Magic is wonderful, mathematics are dull, and Miss Hilton has all but given up on trying to teach me to draw."

"Does Lady Eston think you're on track to have a Season in town? I haven't forgotten my promise."

Bee sighed and slumped back against a tree. "Nothing I do pleases her, *in* the schoolroom or *out*. She would be happier without me around."

"What do you mean? That can't be true."

"It's obvious she prefers when it's just her and Papa in town, and I'm nowhere nearby. Anyone can see it. Ask Harry."

Winston turned to the groom.

"I won't speak about my lord and lady," Harry said. Then he caught Bee's eye. "But others do, and I've heard things. Miss Snow's not wholly wrong."

Bianca rolled her eyes at the meager support.

"What can I do?"

Winston's frown of concern warmed Bee like nothing had in months. "Nothing. There's nothing anyone can do… unless you've changed your mind about sparring?" she added hopefully. He gave one tiny shake of his head, and she shrugged. "I just have to wait her out, I guess. Once I'm eighteen, I'll go to London, and we'll see what happens then."

"You'll go to London, and I'll take you to every cathedral and museum and park you could wish to go to."

"I look forward to that."

"No more than I do."

***

A few days later, Bee overheard the housekeeper telling Miss Hilton softly that Mrs. Cole had made an extra large batch of biscuits filled with her homemade blackberry jam, and to come down to the kitchen if she wanted one later. Bee wanted one. Mrs. Cole's blackberry jam biscuits were her favorite of all the cook's sweet creations. She fidgeted through her

CHAPTER 10

remaining lessons until she was released for the day. Sneaking into the kitchen, she immediately saw plates of biscuits laid out on a table. Bee slipped through the quiet kitchen and froze, her hand extended. Beside the biscuits lay a big, glorious apple pie. It must have just come out of the oven because steam rose thick from its flaky, golden lattice. Caramelized sugars oozed between the woven strips. The smell was so heavenly that Bee couldn't move. All she could do was breathe.

"What in heaven's name do you think you're doing?"

The cook's sharp voice came from the door to the pantry. Bee spun round, eyes wide.

"You were about to steal my pie! Admit it!"

"N-no," Bee protested, startled into stammering. "I would never steal a pie."

"Like hell you wouldn't," Mrs. Cole hissed, advancing on her. Her flushed cheeks were an angry red. "You've been nicking food from my kitchen for years! I've let it slide so far, but I won't have this!"

Bianca recovered, straightening her spine and staring down the infuriated cook. "What would I do with a whole pie?" she demanded. "I've only ever stolen biscuits and scones and things—and only when I can see there's plenty to spare. I'd never steal something that could get you into trouble."

"Then explain what you're doing here, Miss Snow." Mrs. Cole's fists plopped onto her hips.

"I came to nick some biscuits," Bee admitted, scowling at the cook. "Blackberry jam ones are my favorite. I paused because the pie smelled so good, but I wouldn't *take* it."

"That had better be true," grumbled the cook. "Get you off. And if I catch you in here again, you'd better believe her ladyship will hear about it."

Bee shot Mrs. Cole a look that said just how low that threat was and slipped out the back door. Harry was watching for her. He raised his eyebrows at her expression, but said nothing. Bee chose to take the long way to their spot in the woods, trotting around the fields in the hopes that it would help her mood, but instead she stewed the whole way.

"She accused me of trying to steal a pie!" She burst when they finally arrived beneath the trees where Winston was waiting, dismounting while she ranted. "I've never once taken something that big, never once taken something that would get her into trouble. And what do I get? Told off for something I wasn't going to do, and threatened with being turned over to Malorie!"

Winston held out a hand.

"Slow down, Bee. What happened?"

She clenched her teeth and her fists. "I went to the kitchen for blackberry jam biscuits, but the apple pie smelled so good I just had to stop a minute. Mrs. Cole saw me and accused me of plotting to steal it!"

For a moment, Bee thought Winston was going to be responsible and logical and point out that she *had* been about to steal *something*, so Mrs. Cole wasn't entirely without justification. When he was younger, he would have said it, but now he kept any Goody Two-Shoes thoughts to himself.

She couldn't help saying more in her defense. "There's a difference between pie and biscuits."

"Several, I'd say."

"You know what I mean." Bee scowled. "I've only ever nicked small stuff from the kitchen, and only when I know there's plenty. A pie is different. Especially when I heard Malorie specifically ask for apple pie today for pudding."

CHAPTER 10

Winston tried to change the subject a couple of times, asking first about how her lessons went that morning and later if she wanted to see the newest spell he'd learned, but she wouldn't be distracted for long. The unfairness of the accusation stung. She'd always thought she was on pretty good terms with the cook, though she did sneak a snack now and then. But to threaten to tell Malorie! Bee wouldn't see a pastry for a month if her stepmother got wind of this.

Chapter 11

Winston slowed Grayling to a walk as he neared the woods. He usually took the fields at a trot in case there were any rodent holes that could lame the gelding, but today he'd risked a canter. Bee was going to love his surprise.

He hadn't seen her in such a sullen mood in years. The cook's threat to rat her out to Lady Eston had certainly touched a nerve. He wondered if Bee's stepmother was really so terrible or if getting caught and threatened with punishment was the greater hurt.

It should have been simple for her to ask Mrs. Cole for the treats. He could have requested some from the kitchen at home, though their cook at Pinehurst wasn't nearly as good a baker as Mrs. Cole. But for Bee, asking took the fun out of it—sneaking them was a kind of game, one she'd begun after the time she'd tried asking and Mrs. Cole had sat her down at the table and fed her healthful foods instead of the tea cakes she'd been spoiling for.

But the spell Winston had found would solve all that.

Bianca was already sitting in the cave of fallen trees when he rode up. She barely acknowledged him when he dismounted and came over.

CHAPTER 11

"Afternoon, Bee."

"Hey," she said listlessly.

"I found a new spell for you."

Bee shrugged.

"Come on, Honeybee, you'll like this one."

The slight furrowing of her brow was the only sign she'd heard him.

Winston frowned. He'd been hoping for *some* reaction.

He sat beside her and said, carefully indifferent, "Shame. It would have helped you sneak anywhere."

Bee stiffened a little beside him, and he could sense her eyes on him, though he kept his gaze on his hands.

"How do you mean?" she said.

He smothered the grin that wanted to erupt at the interest in her voice. "It makes you inconspicuous, like you blend into the surroundings so well that nobody pays attention to you." He shrugged, as if it were no big deal. "I've only managed to hold the spell for a minute or two, but I'd think that'd be enough to dash into a kitchen for some tea cakes."

"Don't you gammon me, Winston Elliot Graham. Do you really have a spell like that?"

"Of course I do. Have I ever lied to you?"

"I wouldn't know, would I?"

"You would—you've said yourself how bad a liar I am. You see right through me. So tell me: do I have such a spell?"

"Show me." Bee sat forward on her knees and turned to face Winston.

His grin slipped out, and he said the spell-word. Nothing much seemed to happen, but Bee frowned, looking from him to the cave around him and back.

"I can still see you," she said.

"I never said I'd be invisible."

"You said you'd blend in. But at most, your blue coat looks a little more brown. And your eyes are... faded."

"Have you learned about chameleons, Bee?"

"Natural science?" She made a face that expressed how she felt about the subject.

"Chameleons are a kind of reptile that changes color depending on what they're surrounded by. So if one were lying on a rock, it would turn gray, but if it were hiding in a bush, it would turn green to blend in with the leaves."

Bee frowned. "So your spell makes you like a chameleon?"

Winston nodded. "In a way. It doesn't change how I actually look, but it changes other people's perceptions of me. To anyone looking, I would fade into the background and not be worth noticing."

Bee stared at him for a moment, then a smile grew on her face, the first genuine grin he'd seen since her incident with the cook. "Brilliant."

Later, Winston watched Bee ride off with Harry, still muttering the spell-word to herself. She turned and waved just before they were out of sight, and Winston felt that familiar little swell of pride for making her happy again.

***

Bee practiced the chameleon spell as often as she could throughout the day, particularly when she was about to enter the breakfast room or dining room. It was easier to test the results then: if the footman noticed her and pulled out a chair, she needed to work harder. She tried doing the spell when she went out to the stables in the afternoon. Even though Harry was watching for her, he still didn't notice her presence until the spell had worn off after about thirty seconds.

By the end of the third day, the only person who was aware of where she was, even after she'd made herself inconspicuous, was Winston.

"Why are you the only one who can still see me?"

Winston shrugged. "I know what to look for." He looked away as if he were hiding more of the answer.

Bee knew her friend too well to miss this tell. "No lies by omission. What else?"

"Nothing, Bee."

"Winston…" she growled. "Is there some counter spell that you know? Some trick that will get me in trouble if I use the spell around the wrong people?"

"What people do you think you'll be near?" He tilted his head, half laughing. "Wicked magicians are all very well in stories, but you can hardly expect to meet one here."

"You won't distract me," she said firmly. "Why can you see me?"

"Because I *want* to," Winston huffed.

"That doesn't explain anything."

"For most other people, seeing you or not seeing you, it doesn't make much difference to them. For me… it does. I hope and expect to see you when I come out here, and I know what to look for, so I see you." He raised one shoulder. "If you showed up unexpectedly in a lecture hall at Oxford some morning, the spell might hide you even from me, because I wouldn't be looking for you then."

"Oh." Bee supposed it made sense, especially the part about him expecting to see her. Harry would hardly ride into the woods to meet Winston on his own, so she would naturally be somewhere nearby. She wondered briefly if the spell could be expanded to cover another person with her. But she had too many other questions to ask first. "I've been thinking—speaking the spell-word is a dead giveaway that I'm about to do magic, and it could draw attention from whomever I'm trying to avoid. I've tried whispering it, and it seems to work. But is there a way to cast spells silently?"

Winston nodded. "Top level magicians do. That's one of the things we've been practicing at Oxford. It requires firmer focus so that you can hold your concentration and think the spell-word at the same time."

"I'm going to learn that," Bee declared.

"Most magicians can't do it," Winston cautioned.

"Well, I'm not *most*." She planted her hands on her hips and raised her eyebrows at her friend. He just grinned.

So when Winston had gone back to Oxford, leaving what felt like an even greater void in Bee's life than when he'd left before, she began to practice casting the spell silently. She gradually whispered softer and softer until her mouth was barely moving and no one would notice even the slightest outrush of breath. By September, she was back to sneaking treats from the kitchen—always small things in small quantities, of course, and never more than once a week. She'd learned caution, even though she now had a spell that made the thefts almost too easy.

***

Music from the drawing room distracted Malorie from the letter she was writing. Bianca usually practiced on the pianoforte in the schoolroom so that she didn't disturb the rest of the house. If that girl had taken an odd fit to play on a different instrument just to disrupt things...

Malorie left her preferred back parlor and walked to the drawing room, where she stopped just outside the door. It was slightly ajar, giving Malorie a clear view of the instrument. Bianca was there, playing her newest French song, a wistful number about lost love. Malorie winced. While she couldn't fault Miss Hilton's ability to teach the technical skills of music, it was obvious to any discerning listener that Bianca had no love of the art. Her proficiency was improving, but her playing was dull, emotionless. It didn't move the soul as it ought.

And yet, Lord Eston sat just within view, watching his daughter with rapt attention. Perhaps he was a poor judge of music. Or perhaps fatherly affection blinded one to the defects of one's progeny.

Spying silently from the doorway, Malorie decided it was the latter. It had never been a secret that her husband adored his daughter. She'd thought it charming at first, when he'd been courting her, to hear him speak so lovingly of the girl. It had been a good omen, she'd thought, that he would dote on the children that she would bear for him.

But she hadn't borne children. The one miscarriage had been her only moment of hope. Now, watching him adore the daughter of his first wife brought a sick knot of jealousy to the pit of Malorie's stomach. It was bad enough that Bianca was a reminder that the first Lady Eston had succeeded where Malorie continued to fail—bad enough that she was proof that the failure was all Malorie's, as Eston had living evidence that he could sire a child. But that the girl should be the sole recipient of Eston's love...

She'd known that their marriage wasn't about love. It

had been a good match, and Eston treated her with genuine kindness and affection. But she'd hoped—naively, childishly—that he'd grow to care for her. That after some time together, he'd cherish her as the most valuable thing in his world.

Like so many of her foolish wishes, this too had been disappointed.

So she observed father and daughter in jealous annoyance, unable to tear herself from the scene that caused her such pain. It irritated her that he was so blind to Bianca's faults. Not just the mediocrity of her skills and accomplishments—that was nothing. It was her character that was the problem. No matter how much time Bianca spent with Miss Hilton in the schoolroom, there was still a streak of wildness in her. Malorie didn't know what the girl got up to on her afternoon rides, but the hoyden came home with cheeks too pink and eyes too bright to have merely enjoyed a demure ride. But Eston wouldn't listen to Malorie's hints, and so she was forced to punish Bianca in her own small ways.

The last strains of music faded, and Eston sat forward. "That was lovely, snowflake. You're getting better every week."

Bianca murmured something that Malorie couldn't hear.

"I can hear from the song that your French is excellent. How is your Italian coming?"

A groan from Bianca. "Awful, Papa. It's a nightmare. No matter how hard I work at it, I just can't get it to stick in my head. Can I *please* stop? All the lessons are doing is torturing Miss Hilton."

Perversely, Bianca's opposition to the language made Malorie want to enforce her study of it, but Eston clearly disagreed. "I'll speak with Malorie and Miss Hilton."

A rustle as the girl jumped from the piano stool and rushed

over to hug her father. "Thank you, Papa."

Malorie had seen and heard enough. She crept back to her parlor and shut the door, but she didn't return to her letter right away. There was one obvious solution to her problems with Bianca: the girl must be married off as soon as possible. It would take time—she was only sixteen, after all—but Malorie would do whatever it took to speed the process. She would allow Bianca to quit Italian, and she would replace those lessons with additional instruction in deportment. She doubted that she could convince Eston to bring his daughter out in society before she turned eighteen, but she could arrange other opportunities for gentlemen to meet Bianca in the meantime.

Chapter 12

Without Italian, Bianca's lessons ought to have improved, except that she had a new least favorite lesson to replace the old. Malorie insisted on teaching her deportment, which turned out to consist not only of how to behave properly in any situation but also how to plan a party—of every conceivable variety—that would be the talk of the town. Bee hated every moment of it, but she remembered Winston's advice to learn whatever she was taught so that her stepmother would let her have a Season in town, and she bit her tongue and suffered through.

At least these lessons had an inkling of practical application. When Malorie began planning a house party for the beginning of November, she made Bee help her arrange menus and guest rooms, though she steadfastly refused to let Bee see the guest list. Naturally, Bianca distrusted anything Malorie planned in secret. There must be some ulterior motive, and it couldn't bode well for her. But she still looked forward, just the littlest bit, to a break from the tedious routine of daily lessons.

November arrived, and so did their houseguests. Bee discovered she'd been right to be wary: there were six guests, and four of them were unattached gentlemen. Lord Kelly was a widower from Ireland in his late thirties, accompanied by his spinster sister, Miss O'Neil. They both had strawberry blonde hair just on the polite side of red and astonishingly green eyes, but other than their coloring, they were rather plain. Sirs Hargrave and Bellamy were both bachelors on the wrong side of forty, both baronets, and both with brown hair and brown eyes. Hargrave was tall, though not as tall as Winston, with a face like a pug. Bellamy was a tad better looking, but his sideburns were so pronounced that they distracted from the rest of his face.

Bee kept her best polite face on as she was introduced to each guest, despite her growing dismay. As far as she'd been aware, she wasn't supposed to enter society and be married off for at least another year. Malorie, it seemed, had other ideas. The guests milled about the drawing room, talking as they waited for the final guests and dinner. Bee felt the eyes of half the room on her as she attempted to engage Miss O'Neil in a discussion about how the Irish countryside compared to the English.

"I've never been," Bee said, keeping her eyes firmly on the spinster's plain but friendly face. She fought back a blush as she sensed the appraisal—and approval—of the nearest gentlemen.

Before Miss O'Neil could answer, Bee was called across the room by her father, who was greeting their final guests. Viscount Garrison was an old friend of Papa's, a stocky, balding gentleman with an expressive face and a broad smile. He had to be at least fifty, and Bee cringed inwardly as Malorie murmured in her ear that Garrison was recently widowed. She smiled and greeted him pleasantly, and he stepped aside to introduce her to his daughter. Bee could have cried with relief. Miss Sally Clarke was a pretty girl of seventeen, short and full-figured, with light brown hair and the same broad smile as her father.

Bee took her hands and drew her away from the others. "I can't express how delighted I am to meet you," she said. "We'll be inseparable this week, if you don't mind. If you don't like me afterwards, you're welcome to forget about me, but I could use a friend at the moment."

Miss Clarke laughed, glancing around the room, and spoke softly. "I gather the party was not arranged with you in mind."

"On the contrary, I think I was very much in mind—every gentleman here is unmarried."

Miss Clarke's eyes widened, and she laughed again. Bee smiled wryly. "I think we'll get on well, Miss Snow, no need to worry. I'll not abandon you."

"Call me Bee."

"Brilliant. Call me Sally. See? We're already on our way to being particular friends."

Bee wasn't sure how she survived that first dinner seated between Lord Kelly and Sir Hargrave. She couldn't remember ever being more uncomfortable in her life. Across the table, Sally kept shooting her expressive glances that forced her to stifle a laugh. The older girl seemed less than pleased with her own neighbor, Sir Bellamy.

The next morning, the girls arrived in the breakfast room at the same time and contrived to sit next to each other.

"The gentlemen will be hunting this morning," Bee said, having overheard her father discussing it with Hargrave at dinner.

"The weather is supposed to be fine today. Perhaps we could walk out and you can show me around."

"Once it warms up a bit," Bee agreed. "Until then, do you play or sing?"

CHAPTER 12

"I sing a little, but I've yet to find an instrument that suits me."

Bee smiled as she poked at her breakfast with her fork. "What do you say to duets until it's warm enough to go out? It would be a pleasant break from my usual music lessons."

Sally agreed, and they retired to the schoolroom when they'd finished eating.

"The pianoforte in the drawing room is better, but we're less likely to be bothered here." Bee settled herself on the piano stool and shuffled through some music.

They spent the next hour singing together and laughing over each mistake. It was much more fun than practicing alone. This thought was still in her mind when Sally suggested bringing drawing materials out with them on their walk and finding a place to sketch the landscape.

"Do you like to draw?" Bianca asked.

"I love it. I could do it all day if there weren't other accomplishments requiring my attention."

"I wish I did, only because it would make the lessons less demoralizing. I'm a terrible artist."

"Oh, stuff. You can't be that bad."

Bee appreciated her new friend's support, though she knew she was every bit as bad as she'd suggested. But music had been better when shared, so perhaps drawing would be too. Company wouldn't make her a better artist, but the time spent would be more enjoyable. She'd learned that same lesson when embroidering with Lady Rowland, hadn't she? It was strange, really, for someone who had been content to do everything alone for so long, suddenly realizing that she preferred company. She'd always known that she liked having Winston around, but he'd never been there for her lessons, so it had never occurred to her. If only her younger sister and Mama hadn't died, she would have always had a friend at hand.

The girls bundled up and went out, with satchels full of pencils and paper. They wandered through the dull winter garden first, then out through the orchard and up a small hill. At the top, Bee put her hand on Sally's arm and turned her to look back. It was one of Bee's favorite views, when she took the time to look. The orchard stretched below them, still misty in the late morning as the sun only shone weakly through the clouds. The sprawling stone house rose from the mist like something out of a fairy story.

"This is where we'll draw first." Sally plopped herself on the grass, oblivious to the remaining dew, and pulled out her materials.

Bee joined her, and they spent the next half hour drawing the scene. A few glances at Sally's paper gave ample proof of the girl's talent. Bee's own was as feeble as ever—awkward shapes, unmatched sizes, the perspective as wonky as if she were looking at the whole thing through a warped window.

When they'd finished, she showed hers to Sally with chagrin.

"Oh dear, you really weren't bluffing." Sally's cheeks pinked. "I'm sorry, I didn't mean…"

"No, you did, and you were right. I'm awful." Bee looked again at her picture and laughed. "Shall we keep walking?"

They packed up their supplies and enjoyed the rest of their walk, returning to the house when the November chill got to be too much. They settled into the sunflower room with tea and workbags, though not much embroidery was actually accomplished.

That evening after dinner, when the whole company had assembled in the drawing room, the gentlemen pressed the young ladies to show off their talents.

"I do love music," Hargrave said. "Would you play for us, Miss Snow? Miss Clarke?"

Bee shot an alarmed look at Sally. It was one thing to play for friends and family. This would be her first time playing for near strangers. "Duet?" she whispered.

Sally agreed, and Bee ran to the schoolroom for the music they'd shared that morning. She'd thought she was safe from exhibiting her accomplishments as she wasn't out in society yet, but apparently the rules were different at a private house party. Her father and Malorie hadn't objected at any rate. She returned to the drawing room and sat at the pianoforte, beginning with the song that would show off Sally's voice the best. Her friend was due to have her debut season in town next spring, and it wouldn't hurt to let their guests form a good first impression.

The gentlemen went out hunting every morning that week, and Bee spent each morning with Sally, cementing their newfound friendship. The whole group gathered each evening for dinner and entertainment. Card tables were set out the second night, and on the third, Lord Kelly suggested dancing. Furniture was moved aside, and Miss Hilton graciously sat to play for them. They made up four couples, with just enough room to move about. Bee tried to enjoy herself, but no matter her partner, she wished she were dancing with Winston instead. She kept a smile pasted on her face, unwilling to draw Malorie's criticism. She could sense her stepmother watching her. Malorie would expect her to utilize some of the most recent deportment lessons, not simply smiling politely at her partners but innocently flirting. Bee couldn't do it. The thought of batting her eyes at these men who were twice her age made her ill. She passed the evening with a grand effort and collapsed into her bed, exhausted and wishing all their guests would simply go away.

Later that week, the weather warmed enough for Bianca and Sally to sit in the sun on a garden bench. Bee leaned back and turned her face up to catch the golden glow.

"Do you have your magical illusions all prepared for your season?" she asked.

"I have a handful that I feel confident doing. My favorite is fashioning a bouquet of roses—it feels like a kind of art, you know?—but I think every young lady can do that one."

Bee nodded. She'd begun with tulips, but she could now do half a dozen different types of flowers, on their own or in combination. "I like rain," she said. "Especially on days like this."

She murmured the spell-word and rain appeared to fall around them, but neither of them got wet. The sun caught the individual drops and made them sparkle like diamonds. A faint rainbow formed above them.

Sally laughed. "I love it!" The rain faded away, taking the rainbow with it. "Have you tried living creatures?" A spoken spell-word brought a petite bluebird into being on her outstretched hand. It cocked its head and surveyed them curiously with tiny, beady eyes.

"Wow, look at the detail!" Bee admired her friend's creation. "You're an artist even with magic."

Sally beamed and let the bird fade. "Thank you. I just hope someone in town will appreciate it."

"How could they not?" Bee grinned. "If they can't see how incredible you are, that's their loss. They're not worth your time."

CHAPTER 12

Sally laughed and squeezed Bee's hand. "I'm so glad we're friends."

Bianca squeezed back. "So am I."

When all the guests left at the end of the week, Sally and Bee promised to write to each other. The house felt very empty for the first day or two, but Bee appreciated the quiet loneliness for the first time in months. She could be herself without striving for her best behavior. Just to prove the point, she used Winston's chameleon spell to sneak through the kitchen and steal a tea cake on her way to the stable on the following Wednesday. She scarfed the cake in two big bites as she waited for Henry to saddle Diamond for their weekly visit to Pinehurst.

Lady Rowland, of course, was curious how Bianca had enjoyed the house party. Bee found that she didn't want to tell the countess about all the eligible older gentlemen who had been present. While she herself condemned Malorie's taste and judgement in arranging such an event, she was afraid Lady Rowland would include Papa in her censure. Instead, she told Winston's mother about Papa's friend, Viscount Garrison, and his daughter Sally.

The countess considered her thoughtfully. "You've not had many opportunities to make friends of young ladies your own age, have you?"

Bee shrugged one shoulder. Until meeting Sally, she hadn't known what she was missing.

"I'm glad you've made a new friend."

"Speaking of friends," Bee picked up her teacup, "have you had a letter from Winston?"

Lady Rowland laughed. "No, dear, it's only been a fortnight since he wrote last. I don't expect one for another month."

***

At Bee's next deportment lesson, Malorie reflected aloud about the house party over tea.

"I had hoped the gentlemen would show a bit more interest. Garrison admired you, I was sure, but nothing came of it."

Bee was glad that she and Malorie were alone in the back parlor so that no one else could hear her stepmother's matchmaking schemes. She hadn't been interested in any of the gentlemen in question, least of all Sally's father. And she couldn't imagine a gentleman of his age marrying a girl younger than his own daughter. Papa would never agree to it.

That knowledge didn't deter Malorie, however. For the first time, she encouraged Bee to eat more sweets and pastries than even *she* wanted.

"You're still too thin and boyish, Bianca, dear. We need to plump you up—gentlemen prefer wives with curves."

Bee swallowed back bile and refused to eat another bite. In fact, she couldn't look at a tea cake or a tart—or even one of Mrs. Cole's blackberry jam biscuits—for a full week without her stomach turning. She liked her lean muscles and the fact that she could ride for hours and box with Harry without losing her breath. And she didn't much care for the idea of being appealingly curvy if the suitors in question were twice her age.

Chapter 13

Winston was glad that no one was ill this year when he returned home at Christmas. He spent the first evening at home with his parents, but the following afternoon, to no one's surprise, he rode out to meet Bianca.

She was already at their favorite spot, pounding her straw scarecrow target mercilessly. Bee looked up as he dismounted, and her eyes grew round. Her mouth fell open.

"What *happened*?"

Winston bit back a curse. He *knew* he should have refreshed the glamour illusion before he left the house. He cringed inwardly, remembering how bad his face looked: a dark, purple-green bruise spreading across his left cheekbone, some puffiness around his eye, a raw scrape in the middle of the mess.

"I got into a bit of a fight the day before I left." He tried to sound nonchalant, not wanting Bee to worry.

"What did your mother say?"

"She still doesn't know. Your glamour spell works wonders."

Bee's face softened slightly from appalled to an almost smile. "And you're now regretting letting it fade out."

She knew him too well. He shrugged.

"You really ought to ice that." She stepped closer and studied the wounds. "I'm assuming you haven't been, since you're trying to pretend it didn't happen."

Again, she was too perceptive by half.

At his lack of answer, she shook her head in exasperation. "Sit," she commanded, gesturing him to the nearest tree. She pulled a handkerchief from her pocket and looked around. "Do you have any water? I didn't bring any. I suppose I could find a stream..."

"Give it here."

Winston took the handkerchief from her and cupped it in his hands, thinking a spell-word. Instantly, the cloth was dripping wet. He passed it back to Bee before sitting with his back against the tree as instructed.

Her eyes widened again. "What spell was *that*?"

"It's part of a combination of spells, actually. Anywhere I go, I can draw fresh water from our well at home."

"Will you teach me?" She looked back at him and seemed suddenly to remember why she'd wanted the wet handkerchief. She wrung it out a bit, folded it up, and knelt beside him to press it gently against his face.

"I'll teach you any spell I know," Winston said, leaning his head back against the trunk. He had to admit, the cold did feel good.

"So... what was the fight about?"

He'd always been able to talk to Bee about anything, but he had no intention of telling her that. It revealed a few too many feelings that he was supposed to keep hidden.

It had been the end of the final class before the holiday. The professor had been lecturing on connections between various spells they'd learned. Afterward, to make his own connections,

CHAPTER 13

Winston had pulled out Bee's notebook—not just the one he was currently filling, but the first one she'd made as well. It was stupid and sentimental of him, but he felt better when he had it in his waistcoat pocket. The books were still out when class was dismissed, and before he could slip them into his waistcoat again, Tristan had swiped the original notebook off his desk and dashed out the door.

Winston had thrown his things into his bag and followed, cursing Tristan and his constant pranks. He didn't dislike the bloke, but they weren't friends, and this trick wasn't doing his opinion any favors. Winston had shoved his way through the crowd to get at him. His friend Dewey appeared at his side.

"What's up, man? I saw him take it, but why are you bothered? It was the book you filled a year ago, and I know you copy all your spells over into your diary at home."

Winston had gritted his teeth, his eyes locked on Tristan's back, and ground out, "My girl made it for me."

Dewey gave a grunt of understanding. Winston hadn't shared many details about Bee, only enough that his friend knew his heart was spoken for and wouldn't pester him to go out to enjoy the light-skirts.

With an extra burst of speed, he'd caught up with Tristan, grabbing his shoulder and spinning him around.

"Hand it over," he'd demanded.

A teasing grin spread over Tristan's swarthy face. "I think I'll hang onto it a while. Gotta be something important in here if you want it back so badly."

"I'll say it once more, man, hand it over before I force you."

"You? Force me?" Tristan let out a shout of laughter. "Why do you want it so badly, anyway? Is it of sentimental value? I saw the letter it came in—was it a special present from your mama?"

The taunt had been one too many. Winston's fist had struck the other student in the jaw before he'd seen it coming. Tristan had stumbled back but recovered quickly. The fight had lasted less than two minutes, both of them landing solid hits before Winston had sent Tristan to the ground with a strong left hook. He'd crouched and picked up the book from where it had fallen when the fighting began, holding the other man's eyes.

"It's from my girl. And you'll come off even worse if you touch it again."

So, no, Winston would not tell Bee the cause of the fight. He wasn't proud of his show of temper. He shouldn't have let a pranking fool like Tristan wind him up. But he didn't have many things that made him feel close to Bee while he was at university, and he treasured those few.

Bee was holding the cool handkerchief over his injured eye, but she met his good eye and raised her perfect brows, waiting on his answer. He raised one shoulder.

"He took something I valued and wouldn't give it back."

She gave him an odd look, like she knew there was a lot he wasn't telling her, but she let it drop. After a moment, she removed the handkerchief and cast a freezing spell on it. She repositioned it over the bruising, even colder and more soothing now. He let his good eye close, relaxing into the smell of the rosewater she used, the warmth of her beside him. Her gentle fingers rearranged the handkerchief, lightly brushing the hair at his temple. He lost himself for a moment in the sensation.

"Honeybee…"

"Yes?"

Her soft voice made Winston realize he'd spoken aloud. He

didn't know what he'd been going to say. That wasn't quite true. He was a heartbeat away from telling her everything he felt—he'd always felt—for her. Everything he'd promised her father *not* to say for at least another year. He scrambled for something to say instead.

"Will you sing for me? I haven't heard you since we were children, and I'd dearly like to again."

Bee let out a surprised hiccup of laughter. "Sing for you? I'm not sure an aria is quite the thing for sitting on the ground in the woods. And I have no pianoforte out here."

"You don't need one. And you can sing anything at all. No pressure. Here, I'll start."

In his sudden rush of nerves as he tried to cover for his near miss, Winston started singing the first thing that came to mind: a rather bawdy ballad he'd heard at a public house. He could feel the heat creeping up his neck, horrified that he'd chosen such a song with a lady present. But it was too late now; there was no help for it. He pressed on through the verse.

Bee let out a little snort of laughter as he started to sing, and by the time he'd finished the first verse, she was laughing so hard she was hugging herself around the middle and fighting to stay upright. Winston opted not to sing the second verse, which was even more ribald, and grinned crookedly as she pulled herself together. She was still giggling when she froze the handkerchief again and replaced it on his face.

"I'm afraid I don't know any songs like *that*."

Winston chuckled. "I should hope not."

She was quiet for a long moment, her beautiful, dark eyes on the cloth she was pressing to his cheek. Winston stared, mesmerized by the fluttering of those dark lashes, the half smile that tugged those rosy lips. He'd nearly forgotten his request for a song when she began first to hum, then to sing softly.

It was a familiar lullaby, one that Nanny had sung to him, and Bee's Nurse had obviously sung as well. Her voice was low, lilting, wistful. It was a caress of sound, and he knew he'd never forget this moment. Unbidden, a vision of Bee rocking a child to sleep came to him as she sang. A wave of longing crashed over him. Not now, not yet, but someday, he wanted that beautiful little family to be his.

When the song ended, silence fell between them. Winston couldn't think of a single thing to say that wouldn't break his agreement with her father. At length, Bee sat back, dropping the handkerchief to her lap. She examined his bruised face, reaching once more to tenderly brush the tips of her fingers against the edge of the bruise, her touch as light as a butterfly's wing.

"It's getting late," she said. "You should recast the glamour now, before you ride back. And hold ice to it again tonight once Lady Rowland has gone to bed."

Winston nodded, still not trusting himself to speak.

"And I expect you to teach me that water spell tomorrow." Bee grinned at him, her old, fierce grin that always got her way.

"I'll write them down for you tonight so I don't forget," he promised.

Bee stood and moved toward Diamond. Before Winston could focus on the glamour illusion, he caught Harry's eye. The old groom gave him a small smile and a nod. Winston wasn't sure what the man was giving his approval to, but he appreciated it all the same.

CHAPTER 13

***

Bianca waited impatiently for Winston the next afternoon. It was Christmas Eve, so she wouldn't be able to stay long, but she wanted at least a few minutes with him. He'd promised to teach her the new spell, for one thing, and she wanted to give him his gift in person this year.

She'd bought his gift this time, ordered specially by the local bookseller. With how much he'd seemed to appreciate the pocket-sized notebooks she'd made him, she'd considered hand making him something else. But whatever she thought of was either not special enough or was too significant for a friend. She'd have gladly knitted him a hat or mittens or a scarf—that was about all she could manage with knitting, and only if she paid careful attention to each stitch—or embroidered handkerchiefs, but those were things one made for family. Or for one's sweetheart. And however confused Bee might feel about Winston, they weren't engaged.

Although given how her heart had been racing as she'd pressed the cool cloth to his face yesterday, she wasn't wholly opposed to the concept. She couldn't help remembering the tender, almost dreamy way he'd sighed, "Honeybee." If she'd had to guess, she would have said that he'd been thinking of something other than wanting to hear her sing.

But that was silly. He saw her as a friend. His best friend, maybe, but had that status shifted since he'd made more acquaintances at Oxford? He was a university student. She was just a provincial girl, his young country neighbor, who'd never been anywhere interesting.

She sighed. Writing to Sally helped her feel less alone in her mixed up emotions, but it didn't lessen the confusion a jot.

Winston's arrival sent her thoughts scattering to the wind. She examined his face as he approached, frowning as she saw the faint shadow across his cheekbone indicating that the bruise was not fully hidden.

"Don't worry," he said, catching her look. "The glamour's just now wearing off. Mother still hasn't noticed a thing."

Bee shook her head. "You ought to tell her."

"She'd only worry."

"Well, don't expect me to lie about it if she asks me directly."

"You lie about injuries all the time."

"Not to your mother! *My* parents, sure—my freedom depends on it. But Lady Rowland has been nothing but kind to me, and I won't jeopardize that."

Winston raised an eyebrow. "Then I'll make sure not to let the illusion slip so that she never asks."

Bee pressed her lips together. She was hardly one to condemn lying to one's parents, as she'd just admitted. So she shrugged, adding only, "For what it's worth, I'd never lie to *you* either."

This earned a smile. "I know. And you can rest assured that I *can't* lie to you—you see through me every time."

"I don't know," Bee teased. "You're doing it rather brown with the glamour illusions."

He gestured to his face, his smile a little crooked. "I let them lapse for you."

Bee wanted to reach out and brush her fingers over his skin again as she had yesterday, but she resolutely clasped her hands behind her back. "Do you have spells for me?"

Winston pulled a folded sheet of paper from his coat pocket and handed it to her. "As promised. The spell I used yesterday draws the water to wherever you want it, but before it will work, you need the first spell to lock in where the water is coming from."

Bee practiced saying the spells a few times. Winston corrected her and showed her the hand gestures she would need. Illusions were almost entirely cast by spell-word only, so Bee rarely had to combine word and gesture when she did magic. She had to try the gesture a few times, and Winston once took her hands in his to position them properly. Even through their gloves, a spark shot up her arms, and she bit her lip hard.

When he was satisfied that she'd be able to complete the spells herself, Bee folded the paper again and fidgeted with it. There was an awkward pause as they looked at each other. Winston stuffed his hands into his greatcoat pockets.

"I should go," Bee said at last, reluctantly. "Papa will be expecting me. But I have something for you."

She pulled the paper-wrapped gift from her shawl pocket and held it out. Winston peeled the paper off, revealing the small, leather-bound book.

"The shopkeeper said it was about using magic for navigation or location or... I don't know, I didn't quite follow. He said only someone with a university education could possibly understand it." She grinned. "So I thought of you."

Winston's blue eyes twinkled as he smiled. "Thanks, Bee." His expression was hard to read as he looked down at the book and back at her. "Your gift will be delivered tomorrow—I didn't know if you'd be able to carry it home while riding, and I didn't want to cause any real accidents."

Bee laughed. "Now I'm exceedingly curious. Will you give me a hint?"

"I don't spoil surprises." He held her gaze for a long moment, looking like he wanted to say more. But when he spoke, he said only, "You should be getting back. I'll see you soon, Honeybee."

He reached out and took her hand, holding it for longer than a normal handshake. Perhaps he was wishing, like she was, that they hadn't grown up too much for goodbye hugs. Then he let go, and they both mounted and rode away.

On Christmas morning, a servant from Pinehurst delivered a stack of six books bound together with a wide ribbon. Bee recognized a few of them as Winston's old magic textbooks. A card was tucked into the top book: "For Honeybee, In case there were any spells I forgot to teach you. Merry Christmas. W."

A happy warmth filled Bianca as she paged through the books, remembering all the afternoons sitting in the woods doing magic. She took the stack of books from the servant and carried them upstairs herself, arranging them on a small corner table in the sunflower room. She'd gladly spend the winter in the sunny yellow room reading spell books.

Chapter 14

Malorie looked with distaste on the crumpled object on the floor of the parlor. "Where did you find it?"

The groundskeeper kept his down-turned eyes on his clasped hands. "In the woods, m'lady. Same part of the woods Miss Snow rides in most days."

Malorie raised her eyebrows. She'd given both Bianca and her groom strict instructions to stick to the established paths while riding. How long had the girl been flouting her orders? Years, from the weathered heap of rubbishy cloth in front of her.

"You may go. Please send someone to the schoolroom. I wish to see Miss Snow immediately."

The groundskeeper bowed low and left. Malorie frowned after him, considering. She'd been rather liberal in the use of one of her aunt's private spells. When she'd first come to Eston Hall, she'd—naively—thought she'd earn the household's respect and loyalty simply by being the viscountess, and their love by bearing and raising the next generation of Snows. Respect had been granted easily enough, but loyalty… The household was true to her husband first, which was only right, but Malorie should have been next, as his lady wife. But, no.

Bianca, the Eston sweetheart, held the loyalty of the servants much more strongly. This state of affairs couldn't stand, and so, when it became clear that bearing children would be of no use, Malorie had resorted to magic.

It was a simple spell, and relatively harmless. It merely enhanced one's loyalty to the spell caster. She'd thought to use it on Eston himself, but it wasn't strong enough to combat the natural bond between a father and daughter, so she'd opted to win over the staff. The maids and footmen were all hers now, along with half of the grooms and the groundskeepers. She'd used the spell on the cook and housekeeper too, though they had been with the family for decades and their allegiances were not likely to be easily swayed.

Not that she was planning a rebellion. Nothing of the kind. Malorie wanted to support her husband. But she didn't trust Bianca, and she had a nagging suspicion that the girl was always getting up to something behind her back. With magically loyal servants, she had more eyes watching, which had served her well today.

Bianca appeared in the doorway, knocking lightly and curtsying. "You requested my presence?"

"Bianca, dear, can you tell me what that is?"

The girl took in the pile of cloth and straw on the floor. Her expression remained unchanged, but her fair skin paled the tiniest bit. "It looks like a scarecrow," she said quietly. "I'm surprised anyone dared to put such a filthy thing onto the carpet."

"Rugs can be cleaned." Malorie waved the concern away. "I am given to understand that this... scarecrow... was found in the woods, bound to a tree."

Bianca said nothing, her face still carefully blank.

CHAPTER 14

"Is it true, dear, that you ride into the woods instead of staying on the safe paths?"

The girl blinked at her but said calmly, "Sometimes."

Malorie pursed her lips. More than sometimes, if her informants were correct. "Then perhaps you could tell me what this thing really is."

"I believe it really is a scarecrow, my lady, but not intended for frightening birds. Winston has taken lessons in pugilism for nearly ten years, and before he left for university, he used to practice his punches on a straw person like this."

"Why would he keep it in the woods, rather than at Pinehurst?"

"I don't know, my lady. You could ask him."

Malorie gritted her teeth and took a deep breath. The girl was infuriating. "Have you ever boxed with this... thing?"

"No, my lady."

"Never punched the bag of straw?"

"Never, my lady."

Malorie's ire rose. Bianca was obviously lying, though there wasn't a single sign of it in her voice or demeanor. She spoke as if delivering God's honest truth, but Malorie would have to be a blind fool to believe her. She knew the girl's tricks.

"Then, if the scarecrow belongs to your friend, Master Graham, why do you ride into the woods?"

Here there was a flash of some emotion, too quickly gone to be sure she even saw it. "He's my best friend, my lady. As children we created a place to play that was halfway between our houses."

"You rode out to meet a *boy*?" Disgust dripped from Malorie's tongue. She wished she could drum up some horror to throw into the accusation, but she wasn't surprised or shocked by

Bianca's wanton behavior.

"Papa has seen our cave in the trees. He has always known where I ride."

Malorie hadn't thought she could dislike the girl more, but Bianca's cool dismissiveness made her blood boil.

"Very well, Bianca, dear. I hope your friend won't be distressed that his straw figure will be destroyed. He's away anyway."

Bianca nodded. "Will that be all, my lady?"

"Not quite." Malorie turned away from Bianca and the disgusting mess of rotting straw and cloth on the floor. She sat at her writing desk and picked up a pen, twirling it between her fingers. "Your father and I will be leaving for town in a fortnight. You will not be going."

"Seventeen isn't old enough for a Season?" There was attitude behind that smooth tone.

"Not for you. No gentleman would want such an undisciplined, deceitful hoyden for a wife. You're a disgrace to your father and to me."

Malorie half expected to see tears well in the girl's eyes, but instead, her face hardened, and she left the room without a word.

***

Papa and Malorie left for town. Without a child at home, Lady Rowland planned to spend the whole season in town with the earl, rather than joining him for a few weeks later on. Bee was left alone with Miss Hilton and the staff of Eston Hall, just as she had every year. She looked forward to as lonely a spring as ever, but at least she didn't have to put up with Malorie's

CHAPTER 14

caustic remarks. It was getting worse. Even Papa had taken notice once or twice. Her stepmother had always been careful before to let no one overhear her harsh words.

But she was gone, and for a few months, Bee could breathe easy. She'd lost her boxing dummy, but Harry agreed to spar with her a few times a week to make up for it. And she had Winston's books to read when rain kept her indoors. She knew most of the spells, but she found comfort in their familiarity, and in the name scribbled in a childish version of his large scrawl.

Even so, she thought she might have gone mad if it hadn't been for Sally's letters. The older girl wrote every week, describing in detail her adventures among the *ton*. Bee received three full pages about Sally's first visit to Almack's assembly rooms. The next week, she described driving through Hyde Park, and how, at the fashionable hour, so many people turned out that all traffic slowed to a crawl. Morning calls, afternoon teas, card parties, balls… each event was described so fully that Bee began to believe Papa had been right all along not to bring her. Bee hated ceremonious social obligations, and Sally's time seemed to be full of nothing else. Her horse and her freedom suited Bianca better by far. Though she did envy her friend when Sally wrote about visiting the Tower and Westminster Abbey and the British Museum.

Next year, she reminded herself. *Next year I'll see them with Winston.*

As time wore on, though, she sensed a change in Sally's letters. When she'd first arrived in town, Sally had been captivated by the elegance and grace and the whirl of activity, enchanted by London society and having a part in it. A few months later, the gloss had begun to wear off. The ladies were petty and backbiting; the gentlemen lacked one or more of honor, gumption, or intelligence. "I've danced and driven and walked with a half dozen suitors," she wrote, "and not a single one shares my interests. They all pretend to admire my drawings but none of them knows the minutest thing about art!"

Bee lacked experience to offer advice, but she comforted her friend with assurances that there were bound to be gentlemen who appreciated art, and if she was patient, she'd meet one when the time was right. It felt a bit trite, but it was the best Bee could do. She almost wished to be in town with Sally to support each other through the Season together.

Almost, but not quite. She'd see her stepmother again soon enough without wishing away their time apart.

***

If Bianca had hoped that absence would make Malorie's heart grow fonder, she'd have been disappointed when her parents returned to the country. Her stepmother hadn't a solitary positive thing to say to her. Bee found it easiest to avoid her, and she began taking her breakfast on a tray in the sunflower room rather than joining the family. She couldn't avoid them at dinner, but she ate silently and kept her eyes on her plate, behaving as perfectly as Malorie had always wanted, doing her best not to attract notice.

It wasn't a flawless solution, of course, and on the first day of Winston's term break, he found her in the fallen tree cave, sitting with her knees pulled up to her chest and her chin resting on them. She heard Grayling's hooves approach, and then Winston's boots crunching over twigs. But she didn't unfold herself, didn't even bother looking up.

"Bee?" Winston dropped to his knees beside her. "What's wrong?"

She gave a tiny shrug, still not looking at him. "Nothing."

"You promised not to lie to me." His gentle tone softened the accusation in the words. She glanced at him. "Are you hurt?" he asked.

"No." Not in the way he meant.

She could feel him frowning at her for a long time before he spoke again. "What was the last thing Lady Eston said to you? Word for word, please."

"I'd rather not say," Bee whispered. Why did he have to know her so very well? Her throat felt tight, and she thought she might gag on the words if she had to repeat them.

"Bee."

She sighed. He wouldn't let it rest, and she wouldn't lie to him. "'You're an appalling disappointment. I'm glad you're not my daughter.'"

"Oh, Honeybee." Winston turned to sit beside her.

She couldn't bear his pity. "It's fine, really. I can't tell you how glad I am that she's not my mother. I shan't cry over her, so you needn't worry." But her eyes burned, and she glared at the opposite tree trunks.

"Of course you shan't," Winston said lightly. "You have better things to cry about, like how much you've missed me, or how happy you are to see me again."

Bee laughed and leaned her head against his shoulder. One tear slipped past her defenses and slid down her cheek onto his coat. She swiped at it with her hand.

"Really, Bee? I'm only worth one tear?" He teased.

"That's more than I've shed for anything in years, so be

flattered."

They sat together in silence as Bianca got her emotions under control. She suddenly felt too tired to raise her head from his shoulder, and once he rested his cheek against her hair, it would have taken a natural disaster to convince her to move.

"She hates me," she whispered after several minutes. "So much more than before. I don't know what I've done to deserve it."

"Nothing, Bee. You've done nothing. This isn't your fault." Winston shifted so that he could put his arm around her shoulders, holding her close and kissing the top of her head. "You're perfect the way you are. Don't believe a word she says."

Bee could have argued—she indisputably *was* a deceitful hoyden, as Malorie had accused—but Winston's arm around her was too pleasant an experience to ruin with ugly truths.

***

After a long pause to treasure the moment of holding Bee, Winston asked, "Do you still have deportment lessons with her?"

"I never thought I'd wish to take up Italian again."

He huffed a soft laugh. He could imagine very little that would entice Bee to study that language.

"There's a correct way to behave at *every moment*," she groaned. "And it's not just that—she's teaching me to 'flirt gracefully,' too. It's absolute rubbish."

Winston's stomach sank. His mother's letters always included updates from Bee's visits to Pinehurst, and she faithfully repeated much of what Bee told her. For the most part, the deportment lessons sounded like standard good behavior

CHAPTER 14

among the *haute ton*—how to serve tea and plan a formal dinner, how to address people of rank, how and how quickly to respond to an invitation. Flirting, though?

"How do you mean?"

She straightened and turned to face him, and he let his arm fall to his side.

"According to Malorie, if I look at a gentleman like this—" She tilted her head slightly down and to the side so she was looking up at him through her long, dark lashes with a little secretive smile on her pink lips and a faint blush on her cheeks. "—he'll be wrapped around my finger in no time."

Winston gaped at her, appalled. He'd been wrapped around her little finger for years, so such a coquettish look should have had no impact on him. But did it ever. The girl could subdue an army with a glance like that. Napoleon himself would be eating from her hand in minutes.

While Winston could admit that Lady Eston was probably not teaching Bee anything beyond what all mothers taught their daughters in preparation for entering society, it made him feel sick. He didn't want Bee to learn to flirt. Not when he was away at university. He couldn't bear the thought of Bee flirting with a stranger, not when he wasn't around to protect her, not when she didn't even know the power of the weapons she possessed. The girl was playing with fire, and she had no idea.

No, it was simpler than that. It always had been. Winston couldn't bear the thought of her flirting with anyone else. Period. Maybe she didn't feel about him the way he felt about her, maybe he was still just her childhood friend, but thinking of her with someone else made his insides burn with jealousy.

He ached to speak up, to beg her never to use her new skills.

To declare to her how madly he loved her. But he'd agreed before he left for Oxford not to say a word. He'd already known that she was the one for him, and he'd asked her father for permission. It would have been a long engagement, as neither of them were of an age to marry and he still had his education to complete. But it would have allowed them to write to each other, which would have made the time apart more bearable. His mother's letters, while detailed, were never enough.

Her father, however, had refused.

"There's not another young man in England with whom I'd trust Bianca more than you, Graham," he'd said. "I'd be honored to call you my son. But she's much too young. You're both too young. Things change at university. You need to be free to change too."

Winston's stomach had sunk through the floor.

"If you still feel the same when you come of age, we'll talk again."

"I'll see you the day I turn one-and-twenty, sir. Because there's nothing in the world, let alone at Oxford, that could possibly make me stop loving your daughter."

Two years had proven Winston right. He loved Bee more than ever, and it was only with the most supreme effort that he kept himself from telling her that. She'd be eighteen in another six months; he'd be one-and-twenty only a few months later. He only had to wait a little longer.

Chapter 15

To Bee's alarm, Malorie announced over dinner one night in August that they would be hosting another house party in November.

"I ran into Lady Larkwell in town this spring, and she has a bachelor son in need of a wife. I can't say what he'll think of Bianca, but Lady Larkwell's good opinion would set her up nicely for her debut next year." She gave Bee a pointed look.

Bee dropped her eyes to her plate. She wasn't even eighteen yet, and she already felt like she'd been put on the market, without even the benefit of being in town. She doubted Malorie would do her the favor of inviting Sally and her father again.

Bianca's doubts were confirmed when they welcomed their guests. Lord Kelly and his sister had come again, which wasn't a bad thing—Bee liked Miss O'Neil, and Lord Kelly was correct and polite. Lady Larkwell was an imposingly tall woman with a loud voice. Her chestnut hair was streaked with silver, and she appeared ready to render judgement on everything that passed beneath her gaze. Her son, newly made Lord Larkwell, was her opposite. Though tall, he was quiet and unassuming, taking in the world with a dreamy kind of air. Bee wasn't sure what to make of him, but he was friendly enough when seated beside her at dinner.

Papa had arranged for hunting in the morning for the gentlemen, and Malorie sat with Lady Larkwell and Miss O'Neil in the drawing room. Bee would frankly have rather gone hunting than sit with them, where Miss O'Neil was the only one she could at all consider pleasant. Instead, she took her copy of *Arabian Nights* out to the garden to read in the sun and hopefully escape notice for a while. Malorie's matchmaking attempts made Bee miss Winston more than ever, and as she read the book, she could hear him reading it to her as she recovered from winter fever.

A motion along the path startled her, and she looked up to see Lord Larkwell. He, too, seemed surprised to see her.

"Forgive me for intruding," he said. "I didn't expect any of the ladies to come out. It's a bit breezy for delicate constitutions."

"I'm hardly delicate," Bee said. "And I came out because I was equally certain that they wouldn't."

"Ah." Larkwell smiled. "I see."

"I'd thought all the gentlemen were hunting."

Larkwell tucked his hands into his pockets, looking endearingly shy and awkward. "I'm not much of a hunter," he said. "I prefer quieter pursuits." He considered her for a moment. "In fact, I can't help asking... would you let me sketch you?"

Bee blinked at him. "I beg your pardon?"

He gestured to the satchel slung over his shoulder. "I left all of my painting supplies at home, but I couldn't go a week without any art. And you're quite lovely, particularly as the sun shines on you just so. Too picturesque to miss."

Bee had never received such a request before, but she acquiesced. "Shall I stay where I am, or..."

"Stay just as you are, don't move." Larkwell eagerly pulled a charcoal pencil and a sketchbook from his satchel. He sat on a bench opposite, glancing up at her now and then as he began with broad strokes to catch the shape of her face.

"So you enjoy art," Bee said, growing uncomfortable with the silence.

"I do. Do you?"

"Not at all, I'm afraid. But my friend Miss Clarke is quite talented. We drew together once, and she did her best to hide her dismay at my appalling lack of skill."

"I'm sure you can't be that bad."

"That's what she said, before I proved her wrong and she ate her words." Bee laughed. She watched his charcoal dance across the page for a moment. "Do you enjoy visiting galleries, then?"

"Very much. I've always dreamed of traveling to Italy to see the works of the masters firsthand."

Bee remembered Sally mentioning a very similar wish in one of her letters. How disagreeable that her friend should not have been invited this year! The two would have hit it off amazingly.

Larkwell finished the sketch and showed it to her. Even with just a few black lines, he'd captured her likeness remarkably well. Not just her features or expression, but her air. The girl on the page looked as ready to jump up and do something interesting as the real Bee.

"I'm quite impressed," Bee said. "Though it sounds rather vain to admire myself. You're very talented."

Larkwell smiled. "Thank you. You've been an excellent model, Miss Snow. Might you consider sitting for me again before we leave?"

Bee agreed, and added, "I really do think you'd like my friend

Miss Clarke. Will you be in town next spring?"

"Mother will insist on it," he laughed ruefully.

"Then I shall introduce you." Bee got to her feet. "If you'll excuse me now, however, I find I'm getting cold."

"Oh, forgive me for keeping you out here so long." Larkwell hastily stashed his art supplies into his satchel. "Allow me to escort you in."

They walked together into the house, chatting comfortably.

Bee thought the week passed surprisingly pleasantly. The worst part of each day was the evening, when everyone gathered in the drawing room after dinner. Malorie watched Bee with a critical eye, and Lady Larkwell's scrutiny was no less intense. Without any other young ladies present, all displays of accomplishments fell to Bianca. She performed illusions one evening, before suggesting cards the next. She couldn't escape a request to play and sing the following night, however, from Lord Kelly, who declared he had not forgotten her skill and had been wishing to hear a repeat performance ever since. Bee had no choice but to oblige, less comfortable with the task without Sally to share the attention.

When she'd finished, Larkwell approached with a bright smile. "You didn't tell me you could play."

Bee returned the smile. "You didn't ask."

"Forgive my negligence." He bowed and had just opened his mouth to say something else when his mother's voice carried across the room.

"You see? He dotes on her already. I knew they'd make a match of it."

Her attempt at an undertone was as loud as a pronouncement the whole room couldn't fail to hear. Bee bit her lip as Larkwell's whole face turned pink and his eyes went wide.

CHAPTER 15

Kelly jumped into the awkward pause and said something to Papa about his pack of dogs. Bee couldn't see the Irish lord's face, but she could feel his gaze on her. She could have slunk beneath the rug with embarrassment.

"I'm so sorry," Larkwell muttered. "Mama… She… I beg your pardon." He excused himself and crossed the room to join the gentlemen's conversation about hunting.

Bee moved to sit beside Miss O'Neil, schooling her features. She wished more than anything to leave the room, but it was too early to go to bed, and Malorie would have a fit if she left for any other reason. The Irish spinster took pity on her, beginning to speak of books and plays, and after a few minutes, Bee was able to relax again.

Larkwell sought her out the next morning, asking if she'd like to ride around the park with him. Bianca wasn't so sure she wanted to be in the young man's company after what his mother had said, but she did want to ride, so she accepted. Harry saddled up to accompany them. They walked the horses along the trail that circumvented the property, silently enjoying the crisp, sunny day.

When they were well away from the house, Larkwell said, "I apologize again for my mother last night."

"There's no need," Bee assured him. "My stepmother is just as eager to arrange a match for me, if not more so."

He sighed. "I hope you didn't think… Please don't be offended, but I don't mean to offer for you. I think you're wonderful, but…"

Bee laughed at his pained expression. "Have no fear, I wouldn't have accepted you if you *had* offered. I really think you'd be best suited to my friend Sally. And I…" She glanced toward the woods separating the park from

Pinehurst's grounds.

Larkwell may not have known what was beyond the trees, but he smiled and said, "And your heart is already spoken for."

Bee nodded and said softly, "I think so."

"Then we are both content to be friends, and I am extraordinarily glad of that. But I wonder…" He hesitated. "Would you mind if we did not inform my mother of that? She'll be much more bearable if she thinks I'm fond of you. She doesn't hold with the idea of the two sexes being merely friends. I think she'll take it better if I have another young lady to present to her as the potential match she's looking for."

Bee grinned. She could imagine Lady Larkwell being quite vocal in her displeasure, and she wouldn't want to call a tirade down on the poor lord unnecessarily. "I can't see it doing any harm, as long as we're not lying to make it look like you're more interested than you are. We will be friends, and her imagination can take that where she likes. And I shall introduce you to Miss Clarke this spring."

"Will you tell her about me?" He had his customary dreamy, wistful expression again.

"Of course I shall. I tell her nearly everything anyway, but I should be remiss if I didn't give her fair warning that I intend to introduce her to a handsome, eligible, young lord who loves art at least as much as she does."

Larkwell smiled and changed the subject.

Bee was glad when the time came to farewell their guests. Lord Kelly bowed over her hand and kissed it. His expression was difficult to read, and Bee wondered if she was imagining the hint of disappointment in his eyes. Miss O'Neil said she looked forward to seeing Bianca in town for her come out, and Lady Larkwell bid her adieu with more warmth than was really necessary for a weeklong houseguest. But the awkwardness was soon over, and Bee was glad to go back to normal life—once she'd written to Sally, crafting a letter as long and detailed as any her friend had sent to her.

***

The next Wednesday, Bee spent the morning with Lady Rowland as usual, telling her all about the events of the previous week. But when the countess shared her own news, Bee forgot about the house party entirely: Winston was coming home for good.

He'd sent a letter to his mother only a few days before, explaining that he'd managed to get final approval to graduate in December. He'd be returning to Pinehurst to spend some time learning to run the estate with his father.

"He still means to work as a magician," Lady Rowland said. "Rowland is in perfectly good health, and there's no sense in both of them puttering around here, but it would be good for him to learn it all now in case something drastic happens."

Bee didn't care what the reasons were—Winston would be home, and he'd be free to come to town for her entire Season.

***

When Bee visited Pinehurst the third week in December, Winston was already sitting with his mother.

"You're here!" Bee squealed from the doorway, before clapping a gloved hand over her mouth.

Lady Rowland laughed. "He didn't send us word of when he was coming until two days ago."

"I didn't know myself." Winston rose and came to take Bee's hand. He brushed a kiss over the back of her glove and met her eyes. "Honeybee."

Bee blushed at the warmth that rushed through her from his closeness. How was it that the same person who'd allowed her to fight like a boy as a child now made her feel very much like a young woman?

She was grateful for Lady Rowland that morning. Winston's mother called for tea and insisted on Bee joining her on the sofa to sew, regardless of pleasant interruptions. Winston was then called upon to fill them in on everything that he hadn't shared in letters in the last several months. Bee sat quietly and listened, trying to use the annoyance of embroidery to squash the fluttery sensation in her stomach. It didn't work, however, and Bee barely managed a dozen stitches all day.

She met Winston with more composure the next afternoon at their special place in the woods. She wasn't caught so off guard, and she'd thought ahead to nick some honey biscuits from the kitchen to share. They sat side by side on a fallen log to eat.

"I'll be in town with my parents this spring," Winston said.

"You did promise." She shot him a sidelong look. "Your mother mentioned that you'd be finding work as a magician."

"Yes, eventually." Winston tilted his head back to look up at the blue sky between the dark branches. "But my primary goal is to take you wherever you'd like to go."

"As it should be. Your promise has been my solitary light these last few years. I've been dreading coming out ever since Sally told me how it was for her last year—all balls and teas and social obligations—but if you're there it's bound to be all right." She smiled wryly. "Or at least not quite as awful."

CHAPTER 15

Winston laughed and looked down at her. "I can't promise to make all your social obligations bearable, but I can take you to as many landmarks as you like. And I'll dance with you, too, if you'll save me space on your dance card."

Bee let her head rest against his shoulder as she took another bite of biscuit, the honey flavor blooming on her tongue. "It won't seem so very bad if you'll suffer with me."

"And after London," he said slowly, turning his remaining half biscuit over in his hands, "there's the whole rest of the world to see. I'd be happy to take you wherever you like."

Bee stilled, the remains of her last bite dissolving slowly in her mouth because she'd forgotten to chew. This was a very different offer than his promise to show her London. A Grand Tour, or a journey even farther than the continent, would require that they bring a chaperone. Or that they be married.

Could that be what Winston was hinting? Did she hold his heart in the same way he held hers? She lifted her head from his shoulder and looked up at him, searching his face for answers. His blue eyes locked with hers, the beautiful, earth-shaking truth abundantly clear. The flutters that had so often assailed her midsection whipped themselves into a frenzy.

"Would you like that, Honeybee?" he asked softly.

"I can't think of anything I'd like more."

***

The next three months passed in a haze of happiness. Bee turned eighteen. Her father declared officially that this was the year she would have her debut in town, and Winston continued to suggest new sights they could see together, both in London and abroad. Whenever Bee went to Pinehurst for her weekly visits with his mother, which were too habitual now to stop, Winston sat with them in the peony room for at least an hour. For the first time in what felt like ages, Bee had present happiness and the hope of more in the future. At the beginning of March, Papa left for town. He would make preparations for the ladies to join him in a month. Miss Hilton would leave to live with her niece then, and Winston and Lady Rowland agreed to plan their own departure for London the same week.

Bee felt a constant flutter in her heart, an expectancy, an anticipation. She didn't know what London Society would be like, but something told her that this was the Season when her life would change.

Chapter 16

Malorie glared at the letter in her hand. She was clenching it so tightly in her fist that the paper was crumpling. She laid it flat on the desk and smoothed it out, rereading it. It said everything good, everything she'd wanted to read for years: Lady Larkwell was inviting them to dinner at Larkwell House as soon as they were in town to reacquaint Bianca with her son and to introduce her to other select members of the *ton*. Such an introduction to society could only stand Bianca in good stead, starting her debut on firm footing and gaining attention from all the right people. With such a beginning, she couldn't fail to make a match by summer.

How could such a positive letter make Malorie so furious?

She breathed slowly, deeply, searching for the cause. Lady Larkwell was an irritating companion, but Malorie had dealt with far worse. Her son was a weakling, barely more than a boy, but he was rich and titled and would take Bianca far away from Eston Hall, which had always been Malorie's primary goal.

Bianca. Bianca was the problem. As usual.

Lady Larkwell's letter spoke of the girl in such complimentary terms. And if Lady Larkwell introduced Bianca to her acquaintance in town, they were sure to share her opinion. That was the point of an introduction from such a leader in society, after all. Could Malorie sit through an entire dinner party filled with people singing Bianca's praises? Forget dinner—could she bear a Season in town spent listening to others extoll the girl's virtues and pretending that she doted on the little hoyden?

No. It was too much. Bianca had her father and the Pinehurst family wrapped around her finger, and soon she'd have all of London at her feet. The thought was insufferable. It was no longer enough to have miles of distance separating them. The girl had to go. For good.

Malorie sat where she was, staring absently at the letter for hours as she made her plans.

***

Three days until they left Eston Hall. Not that Bee was counting.

She snuck scones on her way out to the stables, thinking it was almost too easy to steal from the kitchens with the chameleon spell. Harry was already preparing Diamond for her ride; his own horse stood ready nearby. Bee barely registered the bags behind his saddle; she went straight to her mare and fed her an apple that she'd snagged with the scones. They mounted and rode slowly from the stable, keeping to a walk until out of sight of the house, just as they always did.

But unlike every other day, as soon as they were out of eyeshot, Harry leaned over and grabbed Diamond's reins from Bee. His knee bumped hers as the horses jostled.

"What are you doing?" Bee asked, startled.

CHAPTER 16

"We're taking a different way, Miss Snow. I need you to trust me."

His expression was too serious to question. Bee nodded. Harry let go the reins then, riding a little ahead and leading the way off the path toward a different section of woods, the woods between the house and the village, not the ones that separated the neighboring estates. Bee followed, mystified, until Harry pulled up and dismounted.

"What's going on?" she asked as she swung down.

"Listen carefully."

Harry stepped close enough to hold onto Diamond's halter, close enough to speak softly so only Bee could hear. His warm brown eyes were solemn and intense, and Bee felt a trill of fear.

"Your stepmother has set a huntsman to kill you. He is watching your usual path through the woods to make sure you never return home. You must flee for your life."

Bee shook her head. None of this made sense. "But if I take a different way—"

"She will try again. She will send another huntsman. She will use magic or poison. You are not safe here."

Bee's lungs squeezed, as though there were no air left in the world. Harry's words sank slowly through her bemused fog. Malorie wanted to kill her?

"How—? Where—?" Her brain couldn't even form a full question.

Harry put a large, square hand on her shoulder, grounding her. "I've brought supplies for you—a bit of money, some food. Enough to get you away from here."

Away. Through the shock, that one word cleared a space in her mind. She'd been wanting to go somewhere beyond

Eston Hall for most of her life, desperate to see something of the world. Now she would get to do just that. Hope bloomed inside her.

"I'll hide for a few hours and then go to Pinehurst," she said, the words coming more and more quickly as her plan formed. "I'll convince Winston to start our travels with a wedding in Scotland—he hasn't proposed officially yet, but he won't say no—and then we'll adventure to some distant shore where she won't look for us. And then—"

"You can't, Miss Snow," Harry interrupted with a shake of his head and a squeeze of her shoulder. "You mustn't go to Master Graham."

Bee felt the wind leave her sails until Harry's hand on her shoulder was all that was keeping her upright. "Why not?"

"It's too dangerous. If Lady Eston thinks you've eloped, she'll hunt you down wherever you go, and she'll have no difficulty tracking the two of you. Your only safety is in her thinking you're dead. I'm about to spin a bouncer bigger than any you've done, and if she sees through me, what's the first place she'll look for you? For your safety and theirs, they can't know anything."

Bee's heart ached. "I can't even say goodbye?"

Harry shook his head. "If there's ever a time when I can safely do so, I'll pass it along for you."

She nodded slowly. She trusted Harry, and she knew he spoke wisdom, but that didn't diminish the pain of relinquishing the plans and dreams she and Winston had spent months crafting.

Harry pulled a bundle from one of the bags behind his saddle and passed it to her. She looked questioningly between it and him.

CHAPTER 16

"Boy's clothes," he explained. "You're too noticeable, and too vulnerable as a young woman. You need to disguise yourself."

Bianca felt numb as she obediently went behind a tree to change out of her riding habit and into the trousers, shirt, and waistcoat. She was already losing Winston; why not the rest of her identity? The clothes fit well enough, and Bee traded her bundled up dress for the overcoat Harry handed her. He held out a pair of shears.

"Forgive me, Miss Snow, but your hair…"

Bee nodded, reaching to unpin the knot of black braids. She untied them, combed her fingers through her mane until it hung long and straight to her waist. She bit her lip as Harry approached and gently sliced it all away, leaving her head feeling light and cold. He stepped back, and she could see the sorrow in his eyes like a mirror of her own. He'd been her most loyal friend for years, second only to Winston.

"How did you find out?" she asked in a whisper. "How did you know that there were men in the household so loyal to Malorie that they'd harm me?"

He shook his head. "She's been using magic to win over the servants for years. I saw it, but I never thought she'd go this far."

"She didn't bespell you?"

The corners of his mouth twitched. "My mum was a magician. She gave me a spell of protection when I took to prize fighting—didn't want me to fall victim to cheating. I've used it every day since, whether I thought there was a risk or not."

Bee nodded. For a moment, she absently stroked Diamond's neck. "What now?" she asked finally.

"Now you walk to the village, catch a ride, and get as far

away from here as you can."

Bee's heart froze at the utter loneliness of it. She couldn't even take Diamond? She'd been lonely before, but for the first time she'd have no one at all.

She took a shaky breath. "Then I guess I'd better go."

She accepted the pack Harry passed to her, stuffing the stolen scones on top before slinging it over her shoulder. She met the groom's eyes one last time. "I don't know how to thank you." Her voice sounded funny, choked and distant.

Harry pulled her close and hugged her fiercely. His voice was gruff. "*Live*, Miss Snow. Your survival is thanks enough for me." He released her and gave her a little shove toward the village.

***

Winston paced the clearing to stay warm. Spring felt farther away than ever in the shadow of the trees. Where was Bee? He'd expected her an hour ago. Maybe Miss Hilton had squeezed in an extra lesson. There had been days in the past when she couldn't come, but none since he'd been home from Oxford, and she'd tried to send a message by Harry whenever she wouldn't make it.

After another half hour, Winston was too cold to wait any longer. He returned home, fighting his disappointment by reminding himself that tomorrow was Wednesday, and his mother had specifically invited Bee for one last coze before her schedule filled up. He managed a tolerable semblance of composure when he returned to the house. The following morning he contented himself with joining his mother in the peony room an hour earlier than usual.

CHAPTER 16

She was planning out what she would embroider on a new pillow and barely looked up from her work. Among all the bits of fabric and silk scattered around her on the sofa were a pair of gray kid gloves.

"What are those for? Surely you can't sew with them."

Mother glanced from Winston to the gloves and back. She smiled. "Bianca left them last week. I'm sure she'll want to pack them to take to town."

But Bee didn't come. Instead, a letter arrived from Eston Hall. Frowning, Mother unfolded it, glancing first at the signature. "Miss Hilton? Isn't she the governess? What could she have to say?" She scanned the letter, growing steadily paler. Her blue eyes flicked up to his for just a moment before she fainted.

Winston was already on his feet. He rang for a maid and Mother's smelling salts. While the servants fussed over her, he slipped the paper from her unresisting grasp and read it over. Two lines in, he stumbled to a chair and collapsed into it, on the verge of needing smelling salts himself.

Bee was gone.

Miss Hilton wrote that Bee had suffered a terrible accident the previous afternoon. The letter was short and devoid of details, only alerting them to the awful fact. It was enough. It was too much. Bee was gone.

Winston remained in the peony room with his mother, who had revived and was now lying on the couch with a cool cloth on her head. The silence was broken only by her weak sniffs and whimpers. Winston was too stunned to weep. He was a statue, cold marble carved into the shape of a man.

Little by little, more of the story was filled in by gossiping servants. Bee had been out riding—on her way to meet him,

Winston thought numbly—when her horse had spooked and carried her off into the woods. Her groom had ridden after her but lost her among the trees. By the time he found the horse, the girl was gone. He'd searched the area, discovering a pile of entrails that he knew to be hers by the shredded remains of a wool riding habit and some bits of raven-dark hair. He'd brought back what he could so that the family would have something to bury.

At this, Winston had to hurry from the room to empty his stomach.

The first part of the story had rung false to him—Diamond had never been skittish. She'd never bolted in all the years Bee had had her. Her only breaks from being a placid mount had been in Bee's fancy, excuses for boxing injuries. This felt like those: a fabricated story to hide… something. But what? And why? Rumors circulated that only some sort of fae beast could have devoured Bee that quickly, and he began to doubt his own doubts. Even the most stolid horse would panic at the presence of an unnatural monster.

Had she truly been torn apart by some creature? Or had she run away?

But why would she run? She'd been happy, hadn't she? She'd been looking forward to finally seeing London. They'd made plans to explore the world together. He may not have proposed yet, but he knew she understood his intentions and returned his feelings.

She wouldn't have left without telling him.

That alone made the monster rumor more plausible.

Now he was a statue with a hollow center, a gaping void where emotion should be.

Mother retired to bed early, and Winston soon followed. He

lay in his big lonely room, the crackling of the dying fire the only sound, staring at the canopy of his bed. It was impossible. It must be a horrible dream. Soon he would wake and find that it was Wednesday and Bee was coming to visit. Her face swam in his mind, her dark eyes and fierce grin, her gentle wistfulness when she'd sung a lullaby, the pink of her cheeks as she blushed.

"Honeybee," he whispered, and the marble encasing him cracked. He suddenly felt too human, too raw, and sobs poured out. He'd never wept like this in his life, but if there was ever a person who deserved it, it was Bee. He sobbed until he was a dry, empty husk, fragile enough for the wind to carry away. The sky was beginning to gray as he finally fell asleep, head and heart aching.

Chapter 17

London was nothing like Bee expected.

The air was thick, heavy, smoggy, and everything she saw was coated in coal dust and dirt. By this point, so was she. She'd spent the past three days on the road, taking part of the trip in the back of a wagon before paying for a place atop the coach to London. She didn't know what she hoped to accomplish by coming to town. But Papa was there, and he was the only one who could do anything about Malorie. And if Malorie decided to hunt her down, as Harry feared, at least she'd have seen something of the world.

Bee meandered down cobbled streets, eyes wide. Lamplighters were about, but the meager illumination did little to banish the oncoming dark. Bee felt more vulnerable than she ever had in her life. She slunk down a narrow alley and huddled in a shadowed corner, hoping to achieve invisibility. She was grateful to Harry for the boy's clothes and for the boxing lessons—at least she wasn't entirely defenseless.

As she tried to get a little rest, her stomach ached. She'd run out of food on the journey, despite her efforts to make it last. She'd never experienced true hunger before, and it was awful. But not as awful as learning that her stepmother intended to murder her. Or as painful as running away without being able to see Winston one last time. Compared to those, the gnawing pangs of an empty belly were bearable.

She sighed and rested her head against the rough brick. Her hair was back to normal by now—short, but normal. Before she'd entered the village that first day, she'd pictured Winston's dirty blond hair and Harry's brown eyes, casting the spell by the reflection of a farmer's pond. She'd maintained the glamour illusion ever since. No one would connect a blond boy with the raven-haired daughter of the Viscount of Eston. But now she was tired and hungry and needed to rest from the magic.

Bee dozed fitfully through the night, waking with the dawn and the early bustle of London life. It was so *noisy* here. Bee rose, stretched, recast the glamour illusion, and left her hiding place.

She used one of her precious few coins to purchase a pastry for breakfast—the smell as she passed the bakery was too much for her empty stomach. She inhaled the pastry in two bites, manners forgotten, then asked the baker's boy how far Mayfair was. He laughed in her face and told her she'd be walking all day because she was on the wrong side of town. He muttered something about country fools as he walked away, and Bee felt a pinch of nerves in her gut. She was too obviously new to town, and she worked hard to look less awed and overwhelmed as she walked on. She studied the way the people around her carried themselves, some with hunched shoulders and tired eyes, wary and cautious. Adopting a similar posture herself, Bee walked aimlessly. She had to get to Mayfair to find Papa, but she didn't know the direction, and she didn't dare ask. There must be carriages she could hire—Winston had told her once, years ago, about hailing a hack—but she didn't know how to go about it.

After hours of walking, Bee finally broke down and asked a shopkeeper which direction Mayfair was. He narrowed his eyes at her.

"You don't look like a toff."

"I'm not," she lied. "But I have a message to deliver."

Something about her accent must have supported her story, because the shopkeeper's suspicion seemed to lessen. He pointed ahead and a bit to the left.

Bee walked on. She spent another night in a dark alley, alarmed by how much activity occurred on the streets at night. Voices and movement woke her every half hour: drunks stumbling home from the tavern, women with boldly colored dresses and painted faces inviting company, stray dogs fighting. Bee huddled within her coat, shivering, wishing she'd chosen to flee to anywhere else in England.

By the middle of the following morning, the buildings she passed were grander, cleaner, and better maintained than the rest she'd seen. Sure she was finally in the right part of town, Bee refreshed the glamour illusion and asked a passing footman where she'd find Lord Eston's house on Park Street. She received the same narrow-eyed scrutiny, and she explained that she had a message to deliver. The footman raised a haughty brow, but he gave her directions.

Bee thanked him with a lighter heart. She was close. Now all she needed was to tell Papa her story, and he would make everything right.

She paused in front of the house when she found it. It was built elegantly of white stone, but it was so very small compared to Eston Hall. It was hard to believe that this was where Papa and Malorie lived every spring, that this was the house she'd longed for years to visit. It was… unimpressive. She debated knocking on the front door, but Papa's town servants wouldn't know her, and even if they knew her name, she hardly looked like a Miss Bianca Snow at the moment. Instead, she made her way to the mews in back, catching up to a stable boy who was sweeping the yard.

"Is this the home of Lord Eston?"

The boy eyed her warily. "Why do you want to know?"

"I've got a message for him." At his continued frown, she added, "About his daughter."

"Already got that message, din't 'e?" the boy said, returning to his work. "On 'is way back to the country."

"He's gone?" Bee's heart sank.

"Left yesterday." He gave her another sharp look. "Don't you get any ideas, though. House is still well guarded even if the master ain't 'ome."

"I would hope so," she said faintly. "Thank you for the information."

Bee trudged away from the house and down the street, paying little attention to where she was going. Papa had been her one hope in this, but he was gone, back with Malorie.

What was she to do now?

A wide, green park opened in front of her, and she wandered through it. It was good to see grass again, and flowers. Bee found a tree to rest against, wracking her brain to come up with a plan. She was in London. She had next to no money. No place to stay. She closed her eyes and rested her head back against the trunk. Who else did she know in town?

She remembered Lord Larkwell had told her that he'd be in town this Season. Perhaps he was already here? She could go to him and possibly stay a night before borrowing the fare for a ship's passage to... somewhere...

She shook her head slightly, still resting against the tree. No. Lord Larkwell lived with his mother, and Lady Larkwell would be sure to tell Malorie. They would be no help.

But Sally might be, if she was in town already. Her father, Lord Garrison, was a friend of Papa's. Bee hoped he'd be capable of keeping a secret, but even if he did tell, he'd tell Papa, not Malorie. And maybe she could convince Sally to covertly send a message to Winston for her.

Bee smiled. It might take her another day or two to find out where Sally lived, and who knew whether she was even in London yet, but it was something. Now, if she could just find somewhere to stay a night or two so she wouldn't be sleeping on the street again, her plan would be complete.

***

As Bee left the park, she nearly tripped over a boy crouched on the street.

"Oy, watch it!" He glared at her through a short curtain of dirty brown hair.

"Sorry," Bee said. "Didn't see you." She stepped back, then noticed what he was doing.

The walkway was built of wide stone pavers rather than cobbles, and he was drawing on the stone with a stick of charcoal. A hat sat beside him containing a few small coins from impressed passers-by. Bee was impressed too: he had drawn a perfect copy of the park she'd just left.

"You're good," she said, studying the boy.

He glanced up at her again. "Thanks."

Bee was terrible at guessing ages, having not been in company with any children since she and Winston had been children themselves, but she didn't think he could be more than ten or twelve. His shirt and trousers were a bit loose and his boots were worn almost through. A black streak crossed his face where he'd obviously used his dirty hand to push his hair from his eyes. Bee wondered if he'd be any help.

"What's your name?"

He sat back on his heels. "What d'you want?"

Bee shrugged. "To talk. I'm new to town."

He looked her over and grunted. "Toff talk, flash togs. You a runaway?"

"Maybe." Bee scowled at him. "Know the names of anyone who lives in these houses?"

"Nah." The boy waved dismissively. "Too grand for the likes o' me."

Of course finding the home of Viscount Garrison wouldn't be so easy.

"You live in one of 'em?"

"Nah," Bee echoed his word. "Don't know who owns them, but I've got a message to deliver to someone and don't know where to find them. No hurry though." Bee's nerves screamed that that was a lie—now that she had an idea of whom to look for, she wanted to find Sally immediately—but she thought a nonchalant attitude would stand her in better stead with this kid. "Know anywhere I could stay a night or two? Preferably free? And indoors?"

She shoved her hands in her pockets.

The boy looked her over again. "Name's Davy," he said finally. "I may know a place, but you gotta get past Grim."

"Who's Grim?"

"The oldest of us. He says whether you can stay."

"Why's he called that?"

"Ain't never seen him smile."

A boy named Grim sounded intimidating, but Bee wasn't deterred. "How do I convince him?"

He shrugged. "There are seven of us, and the little ones can't do much yet but beg. You nick enough food for the lot, and he won't turn you out."

Bee's stomach knotted. Steal food? Was she truly reduced to petty thievery? But she didn't have many options, and staying with others indoors had to be better than staying alone on the street. She considered the boy in front of her as he went back to his drawing. Seven kids, some younger than Davy, all hungry. Bee's heart softened. She now knew how hunger felt, and the thought of children feeling like that every day made her want to do something. Even if she only brought them food this once, she'd have made a difference.

"Fine," she said. "I'll do it. But I don't know my way around. Where's a market? How do I find you again?"

"I'll come along." Davy pocketed his charcoal and the coins and slapped the hat onto his head. "Gotta witness this."

He led her silently but quickly along the streets of Mayfair until they reached the edge of a market square. There, he lounged against one of the buildings, looking lazy, bored, and innocent.

"Think you can handle it?"

Bee darted a glance around the market, taking in the stalls, the crowd, the exits. She nodded. "Where do I find you again?"

"I'll wait a block back that way." Davy jerked a thumb over his shoulder. "And remember—seven people. Plus you, if you want to eat."

Bee's stomach ached. Oh, she wanted to eat. Taking a deep

CHAPTER 17

breath, she told herself that this was just like nicking pastries from the kitchen, and more urgent, because the food was for kids who were actually hungry. She thought the spell-word for the chameleon spell and slipped from the shadow of the buildings and between the stalls.

She'd planned her route as well as she could with her limited view. She pocketed a couple of apples from a fruit stall first, then three meat pasties and a loaf of bread. Her heart was pounding too loudly in her ears for her to count down the seconds. She couldn't risk the spell wearing off before she was away from the market, so she slipped down a side alley and found her way around to where she was supposed to meet Davy. He wasn't there yet; Bee assumed he'd stuck around to watch her. What had he seen? Winston was the only one who had knowingly witnessed her using that spell.

After a few uncomfortable minutes spent hovering in a dark alley, Bee saw Davy. She slipped out and fell into step beside him.

"Where to now?" she asked.

He started and bit back a cry of shock before muttering a curse. "What was that? You disappeared!"

Bee shrugged. "A bit of magic. Couldn't have gotten as much without it." A sick feeling had lodged itself in her stomach. She'd never stolen this much at once, and never from innocent shopkeepers. Taking food from the kitchens at home was hardly stealing. This was different. She forced the feeling back. "So, are you going to take me to the others now?"

"What's your name?"

"Ben," Bee said, saying the first boy's name that was at all close to hers. "Ben White."

Davy nodded and led the way through a series of back streets.

Bee followed, carefully hugging the food close inside her coat. The pasties were warm against her side. She tried to memorize landmarks as they passed, but she was still completely lost by the time they left the better neighborhoods. A few more turns took them to a rundown street of sagging grayish buildings that seemed to hold each other up after a drunken night. Davy led her to a rickety stairway in the back of one building, up and up, until it ended just below the attic. He leapt up, grabbed the sill of the attic window, and hauled himself in. His head poked back out to look down at her.

"You coming?"

"Take these." Bee passed up the pasties and the loaf of bread so that her hands would be free. Davy disappeared from the window. Bee was taller than the boy, so the jump to the window wasn't too far, but she'd never hauled herself through such a small gap before. She heaved herself up and slithered over the ledge.

The room she found herself in was dark and low, with a slanted roof. She got to her feet, catching her bearings as voices clamored nearby. Her eyes adjusted until she could see Davy at the center of a small crowd of younger boys, all of them talking at once.

Everyone fell silent as another voice spoke from the corner. "Who's this, Doodles?"

The voice had that awkward timbre between a boy's and a man's, not cracking anymore but not as deep as it would become yet. Davy looked into the shadows.

"Ben White. Needs to kip somewhere. Offered 'im a place if he could grab food for the lot."

Bee couldn't see the figure in the corner, but she noticed that Davy spoke with the deference of respect, not fear. Movement

CHAPTER 17

drew her attention back to the shadows. A tall boy emerged from the darkness, his own skin the color of coffee without cream. His dark eyes were sharp and inquisitive. He couldn't have been more than fifteen, but he was the oldest of the group and the obvious leader.

"Are you Grim?" Bee asked.

He nodded silently, still studying her.

"I'm new to town," she said quietly. "I don't know my way around. But as Davy can attest, I brought food for everyone, as much as I could safely take." She pulled the apples from her pockets and tossed them to him. He caught them deftly.

"A greenie bumpkin couldn't nick so much without getting caught." He raised a brow disdainfully.

"I may be a bumpkin, but I'm not wholly unused to theft." The sick feeling in her gut was back.

"And 'e's a magician," Davy put in. "Vanished soon as he stepped into the market. Turned up two minutes later with 'is arms full."

This earned Bee a round of eager questions from the younger ones and grudgingly admiring consideration from Grim.

"Right," the oldest boy said. "You can stay. Jack, divide the food."

One of the younger boys whipped out a pocketknife and started cutting everything up. As he did, Bee was introduced to the rest of the group. Grim and Davy she knew; the Twins, who apparently did everything together and didn't answer to individual names, were a pair of freckled redheads of about eight years old. Jack, who was cutting the food, and Squid, who crouched next to him, both had dirty hair somewhere in the dark-blond-light-brown range. And Johnny, the youngest, couldn't have been more than five. He had angelic, white blond curls and the bluest eyes Bee'd ever seen. He crossed his skinny arms and regarded her with surly distrust from across the room.

Once the food was split up and shared out, everyone devoured the meal in seconds. Bee hardly felt like her hunger was sated, but at least her stomach wasn't as empty as it had been. The Twins started hounding her with questions as soon as they'd swallowed.

"Where you from? Whatcha doin' 'ere? You a proper magician, like?"

Bee answered carefully, explaining that she'd grown up in the country but she'd run from home. "I'm not a true magician," she said, thinking of Winston's years at Oxford. "I know a handful of spells." It was an understatement, but she didn't want the boys to think she could solve all of their problems with magic.

"You talk like a toff," Squid called from his seat across the room.

"Said your name is White?" one of the Twins added. "Like that posh gents' club?"

Bee had heard of White's, of course, one of the clubs where gentlemen of the *ton* could place wagers, smoke, read the paper, dine, and discuss politics. Papa belonged to one, though she wasn't sure which. "Not related," she said.

It didn't matter, apparently. Once the idea was planted, the name stuck. She talked like a "toff gent," so she would be Whites for however long she stayed with this crew.

Chapter 18

The groom's story didn't sit well with Malorie. It was too convenient. A tragic accident on the same day that a huntsman waited to shoot her down? Unlikely. But she couldn't deny that the ragged scraps of fabric had come from Bianca's riding habit. She'd noted the dark blue as she passed Bianca in the hallway so that she could tell her huntsman what to look for. And the lock of silky black hair had obviously come from the girl as well.

Even so, it was suspicious.

Malorie had been prepared to play the part of devastated parent, so she went along with what she'd planned, with one slight alteration: instead of locking herself into her bedchamber to indulge in hysterics, she chose to wander the house and grounds, as if her grief proved too restless to remain in one place. While this brought her into contact with too many members of the staff who were genuinely mourning the loss of the viscount's daughter, it also allowed her to find her way to the stables to see Bianca's horse.

A groom was at her side before she even made it through the stable doors, one whose name she didn't know but whom she was certain she'd spelled to loyalty.

"This ain't the place for a lady," he said with a bow. "May I escort you to the house, ma'am?"

"Oh, but I'm here to see the horse... *her* horse... I just wanted to see..." She forced a fake sob.

The man led her inside, solicitous, compassionate. He showed her the mare, Diamond, who tossed her head and rolled wild eyes. "Best not get close, my lady. The poor girl's had a scare."

"Indeed," Malorie said softly. Diamond was as skittish and unsettled as one might expect a horse to be after having her rider snatched from her back and eaten. Perhaps her suspicions were unfair, and it was all the oddest coincidence.

As Malorie left the stables and returned to the house, she hid a smile. By huntsman or by beast, Bianca Snow was gone.

***

Winston stayed in bed for the first three days. Once his stony shell cracked, memories crowded in, overwhelming him. Teaching Bee spells. Sparring. Watching her lying in bed with winter fever. Reading to her. Climbing trees together. Her gentle fingers as she iced his bruise. Seeing her for the first time after a term at university and feeling like he could finally take his first full breath in months.

He remembered the first time he'd met her, when he was six and she was just three, as clearly as if no time had passed. Her parents had come for dinner, and they'd brought her along for the first time, since her nurse was unwell. Nanny had gladly watched both children in the nursery, and Winston had been fascinated by the tiny girl. She'd been a little whirlwind, into everything and full of questions. At last, she'd worn out, and to stave off the whining, Winston had read to her from a book of children's fables. She'd fallen asleep on his bed. He'd thought she looked like an angel sleeping there, with her long, dark lashes feathered over her cheeks. He'd been in love with her ever since.

On the second day, his father came to see him, sitting heavily on the edge of his bed. Winston couldn't look at him. He didn't want to see disapproval in his father's face, didn't want any suggestion that he should buck up and be a man in the face of the hardest loss he'd ever imagined facing. So he stared up at the canopy, silently waiting for the earl to speak.

"This loss is hard on us all," Father said finally, "but hardest on you. Take the time you must, son."

This was so far from what Winston was expecting that he darted a glance at his father. Father wasn't looking at him; he was frowning instead at the untouched breakfast tray on the table.

"I would ask you, however, to exert yourself to eat. Your mother bears her own grief—please don't make her worry about you as well."

"Yes, Father." Winston's voice was a hoarse whisper, but it was enough. His father rose from the bed and went to the door. He paused there and turned back.

"I'll send someone with a new tray. Do your best with it."

When he was gone, a servant came to replace the tray. Winston ignored them. After he'd been alone again a long while, he raised himself on his elbow and poured himself a cup of tea. He didn't bother with sugar: his whole life was bitter now, why should his tea be any different? The plate was loaded with toast, scones and jam, and bacon. He choked down the bacon and toast, but he couldn't face the scones. Sweet things reminded him too much of Bee.

On the day of Bee's funeral, he forced himself out of bed, into clothes, and downstairs. Mother was in the peony room, gazing absently at the fire. She was in the muted shades of half mourning, as befit a friend of the family, but she seemed unsurprised to see him in the black of full mourning. She reached out a hand; he took it. They sat together in silence until Father came in to announce that the carriage had been ordered to take them to the church.

The small parish church was packed full, and Winston chose to stand at the back rather than sitting with his parents in case he needed a quick escape. He nearly did walk out when the parson began speaking. Had the man ever *met* Bee? He droned on about an excellent student and dutiful daughter, which was utter rubbish. When he called her a loyal friend, he hit—however accidentally—on the truth. He said she'd been full of life, and that, too, was true—Bee had always been the very epitome of not dead. Winston swallowed hard. He managed to keep himself in the church, but only just. As soon as he'd given Lord Eston his condolences, he was out the door, striding along the road toward Pinehurst. His parents could pick him up on the way, or he could walk the whole way, it didn't matter. The fresh air might do him good.

The next morning, Winston got up and dressed again. Somehow, the time for wallowing was over, though he had no ambition to do anything. He ate a small breakfast, wandered the grounds aimlessly, then joined his mother in the parlor again. She sighed.

"The world seems so dull now," she said. "But I suppose I ought to..." She reached for her workbag and began pulling out the cushion she'd been designing. With a choked sound that blended a gasp and a sob, she took the gray kid gloves from the bag, Bee's gloves that had been left behind. "I'd forgotten…"

All the pieces of her project must have been shoveled back into the bag without ceremony when she'd gone faint at the news; Winston couldn't remember. Now he stared at the gloves, stricken. With a sniffle, Mother got to her feet and carried the gloves to the desk, where she opened a filigree box and laid the gloves inside.

"Call me sentimental," she quavered, "but I can't… You don't think I should…?"

"Keep them." Winston worked so hard to keep the surge of emotion inside that his voice came out entirely flat.

Mother nodded, sniffled again, and shut the lid. She dabbed at her eyes with the end of one sleeve. Winston stood, pulling a handkerchief from his pocket. He handed it to her and helped her back to her seat, where she proceeded to cry into his shoulder. Tears streamed silently down Winston's face too, and he didn't bother to hide them.

***

The attic room was crowded with eight of them, but everyone shifted a bit to make room for Bee to sleep. When the sun went down, Grim lowered a tattered wool blanket from where it was nailed above the window so that it hung over the opening. It didn't keep out the cold, but it was better than nothing. Bee huddled in her coat in a corner and fell asleep, feeling safer now that she was off the streets. A small room full of people was still noisy, even when those people were asleep, so she startled awake many times through the night. But it was better sleep than she'd had since leaving home.

When the drab morning light peeked around the curtain, Bee

sat up. She could see that most of the others slept in tangled up heaps to keep each other warm. Johnny snuggled close with the Twins, and Davy was lying every which way with Jack and Squid. The reason for this was clear: there weren't enough coats and blankets between them, and what they had were threadbare. Only she and Grim slept alone. Grim was still curled in the corner closest to the window, his wool blanket looking somewhat newer than the others'. She supposed that as the oldest, he took it upon himself to be the first line of defense if anyone tried to break in. Or else he wanted to be closest to the exit if they ever needed to make a fast escape. She frowned. Having only known the boys for a few hours, it was hard to tell.

The waking up sounds of London crescendoed, not muffled in the slightest by the blanket over the window, and the boys woke and stretched. A bit of good-natured shoving and tussling happened as they straightened themselves out.

"Watch who you're kicking at night," Squid grumbled to Davy as he rubbed his shin.

"Tomorrow Johnny sleeps beside you," one of the twins muttered to the other. "'E's all elbows and knees, and they're sharp."

There was no food to be had for breakfast, so once everyone was awake, they began to scamper out the window and about their business. Bee wasn't sure what that business was, and wasn't sure she wanted to know, but she had to do her part if they were going to let her stay until she'd found Sally.

"I don't know my way around," she murmured to Davy as she watched Grim, Jack, and Squid swing themselves out the window and drop onto the stairs. He looked up at her as if he'd forgotten she were there, or maybe he'd forgotten she was new. He hailed the twins before they disappeared out the window.

"Whites'll follow you two today. Don't lose 'im."

The twins rolled their eyes as the first one dropped out of sight. The other jerked his head for Bee to follow before doing the same. She clambered out the window and dropped heavily onto the stairs, then rushed down them after the twins. Davy and Johnny followed before disappearing together down an alley going the opposite direction.

"Where's everyone going?" Bee asked breathlessly as she tried to keep up with the scampering twins.

"Each to 'is own lay," one of the boys said. "Doodles takes Johnny to a safe place to beg, then Jack and Squid pick 'im up on their way back later. We're off to Bond Street."

Sally had written to Bee about shopping in Bond Street. It was where the *beau monde* fitted itself up to be seen. She thought about Davy drawing on the flagstones and Johnny begging, and she wondered aloud what the twins did to get money.

"We're cloyes, ain't we? Regular bulk and file—best way to get the blunt."

Bee had no idea what that meant, so she determined to figure it out for herself. They paused in an alley that opened onto Bond Street. The twins instructed her to stay in the shadows, out of the way, then melted into the crowd.

At first, Bee was distracted by the fine carriages and elegant people on the street, engaging in polite conversation as they went about their business, oblivious to the dirty girl dressed as a boy in the shadows. She should have been among them, having her first gown fittings by a London modiste. Instead, she tore her eyes away and searched for the twins in the crowd.

They were hard to see, but she caught a glimpse of them now and then. She couldn't tell what they were doing until she saw them pushing their way through a group almost directly in front of her. One of the twins collided with a gentleman and ran off, while the other bumped him more gently, patting his arm and apologizing before haring off after his brother.

Suddenly it hit Bee with perfect clarity: they were pickpockets.

She retreated farther down the alley. They'd been at it for a full half hour by now. Surely they'd need to move somewhere else before long. Bee waited and waited, her heart racing, torn between shock at what they were doing and worry that they'd forgotten about her. She didn't know how to get back to the attic room.

The twins returned to the alley, brimming with silent enthusiasm over their successful morning. They took Bee to the nearest market, where they spent their new coins on bread. Bee asked the shop boy if he knew where the Viscount Garrison lived, but he gave her a funny look and a shrug. She didn't have time to question anyone else—the twins were breaking one of the loaves they'd bought into three, and she had to keep up or they'd eat her portion. They scarfed their bread as they made their way back to the attic. The other two loaves they set aside to share with the others that night.

Bianca spent the whole first week following either the twins or Jack and Squid, who worked as another pickpocketing team in a different part of town. She asked for directions to Sally's house whenever she dared, but no one could give her an address, and she couldn't risk drawing too much attention to herself.

She never found out what Grim did during the day, but there

was food in the evenings—sometimes enough, sometimes not, depending on how the thieving had gone. And once Grim came home with two slightly less threadbare blankets to share between the crew.

Bee stayed awake for hours her first few nights, wrestling with herself about the boys she'd fallen in with. She couldn't face the idea of living by theft, but she had no marketable skills like Davy, and she'd never get anywhere by begging, not without that innocent, angelic look Johnny managed. And finding Sally was taking much longer than she'd expected. Without any other options, Bee finally decided that she'd only steal food, and only when necessary. She'd have to find other ways to be helpful.

***

One night, not quite two weeks after she'd joined the crew, a spring storm crashed overhead. None of the boys could sleep. Poor Johnny squeaked and whimpered at every clap of thunder. His jumpiness irked the twins, as he kept startling them and digging them with his elbows as he tried to burrow closer. As the grumbling increased, Bee gave up on sleeping. She slid a bit closer to the mound of wriggling boys and leaned against the wall.

"Once upon a time," she began, softly enough to be soothing but just loud enough to hear over the pounding rain, "there was a king named Shahryar. A rather terrible thing had happened to him, and he didn't trust anyone."

She paused. The boys had stopped squirming, and several pairs of eyes were on her.

"What was the terrible thing?" came a voice.

"His queen left him to marry his brother, who was gathering an army in order to take over the throne."

"No wonder the bloke didn't trust anyone," muttered one of the twins. "What 'appened to 'im?"

Bee suppressed a smile. Like Scheherazade in the story, she would distract the boys until their troubles were over. Fortunately, she'd read *The Arabian Nights' Entertainment* more than once, and she remembered many of the stories. She launched into the first story, continuing until the worst of the storm abated. Then, like Scheherazade, she stopped speaking in the middle of a tale, promising to finish it later.

"Time to sleep now," she said. Johnny was already snoring with his head on one of the twins.

As she settled back down with her coat wrapped close around her, Bee finally decided to stop looking for Sally. Her search wasn't getting her anywhere, and she'd grown fond of these boys. They needed someone to look after them, more than just Grim, who was only a boy himself. No one would think to look for her here, and maybe she could do some good. It wasn't the grand adventure to see the world that she'd longed for, but for now, she didn't mind.

Chapter 19

Winston's mother came to find him on his birthday. It was well past noon, and he was still abed with an untouched breakfast tray on the table beside him.

"I thought we were past the days of refusing to eat or get out of bed," she said, sitting on the edge of his bed and smoothing the coverlet with one hand.

Bee had been gone for more than a fortnight. Seventeen days since his dreams had imploded, since the most important person in his world had left it.

Winston didn't look at his mother. He mumbled into his pillow, "We were. But today…"

"You had special plans to celebrate with Bianca." It wasn't a question. They'd never discussed his one-and-twentieth birthday, but his plans to show Bee around town were common knowledge in Pinehurst. Mother gently stroked his hair. For a few minutes, he lay unmoving and let her comfort him as she had when he was a small child. Finally, her hand stilled. "You loved her, didn't you?"

"I'll always love her," he whispered.

"Sweetheart…"

Winston shook his head. He'd kept his secret inside for so

long, and now it felt like he'd burst, his outer shell breaking apart from the growing pressure within. He rolled to his side, and the words tumbled out. "I asked Eston for her hand before I left for Oxford. He said we were too young, but he as good as promised his permission when I came of age. I've been counting down the days…" He swallowed hard. "I was going to talk to him this morning and then ask Bee. We could have been married by the end of the Season." A fleeting image of Bee walking into a church on her father's arm silenced him.

A gentle sob drew his gaze to his mother's. Tears streamed down her face. "I wished for that," she whispered. "Ever since you were children, I wished for that. She always brought you to life like no one else."

Winston sat up and hugged his mother, and they cried together. Winston had never been one for tears, and now he felt like they were always close by. Surely the well would dry up eventually? Judging by the ache in his chest whenever he thought of Bee, which was nearly every moment, that time wouldn't be soon.

***

By the time Bee had been living with Grim's crew for three months, she knew the back streets of their part of London as well as any of them, and she'd begun using some of their cant phrases, too. For the most part, they'd accepted her presence. A few, like Jack and Johnny, had been more reluctant to welcome her, but after the storm and the storytelling, they'd softened. Now, when Johnny had nightmares, he'd come wake her up and sit beside her so she could whisper stories to him until he fell back asleep. Grim and the twins had gotten on her case about using her magic to pick pockets—that invisibility trick was why they'd let her join them in the first place—but she'd stood firm, and she'd brought enough useful things back to the attic from her foraging that they let up.

She'd found a pair of boots that were worn but not as tattered as some the boys were wearing; one of the twins got those. A pair of gloves with a hole in one finger. A chipped cup and a jar with the top lip broken off. The boys looked at her funny when she brought the last two in, but she used a spell to clean them both, and then she used Winston's water spell to fill the jar with spring water from Eston Hall. She'd done the first half of the spell on the spring the day after he'd taught it to her, and she'd never had a need or opportunity to use the second half. Watching the jar fill with crisp, clean water, Bee was overrun by memories and longing. She forced back the emotion and poured a cupful for each of the boys. From then on, she kept the jar full, and everyone could drink clean water rather than whatever contaminated stuff they found on the streets.

May was nearly over, and the cream of society were beginning to clear out of town, preparing to spend the summer months in the country or at some watering hole or other. Bee spared a thought to wonder what those were like—she'd never been to Brighton or Lyme-Regis any more than she'd been to London.

The weather was fair, and she'd left her overcoat in the attic, going about in shirtsleeves and waistcoat. At first she'd clung to the outermost layer to help hide what few curves she had, but those were long gone. One insufficient meal a day, with a possible extra scrap here and there, had reduced what Malorie called a "boyish figure" to rail-thin ambiguity. Even her monthly bleeding had been absent since she'd left home, banished by stress and near starvation, and Bee was grateful to have one less thing to hide from the boys.

No one from Eston Hall would have recognized her now. But Bee was alive. And she intended to stay that way for as long as possible.

Bond Street was less crowded than it had been when she'd first watched the twins at work. Bee slipped along the alleys, looking for any discarded thing worth taking. She was having an off day with no luck, and she was about to head for a different part of town, when she heard a laugh that sounded familiar. Ducking into the shadow between two buildings, Bee scanned the shoppers for the source of the sound.

With a pang, Bee recognized Sally. The older girl was standing a few yards away, looking graceful and womanly in a pale coral walking dress and matching hat. She was talking animatedly with another lady, whose face was hidden by her bonnet. Bee watched her for a long moment, holding her breath. Sally looked so relaxed and happy. Bee smiled, but it was painful too, this glimpse into a world she didn't belong to anymore. Her plan of asking her friend for help was long discarded, fading further into the distance the dirtier and more ragged Bee got.

Tearing her eyes away, Bee observed the rest of the busy street and received another shock: not far beyond her friend stood Lord Larkwell with another gentleman. At the sight of the young artistic lord, Bee remembered her promise to introduce him to Sally when they were all in town. The introduction would never happen now; the two of them could be steps apart every day and never know that they were perfect for each other.

Bee frowned. That wouldn't do. They were all in town now,

CHAPTER 19

after all, and a promise is a promise. Her gaze darted from one to the other as a plan formed.

With a deep breath and a mental sigh at her foolishness, Bee dashed from her cover. In seconds, she was beside Sally, snatching her friend's reticule and sprinting off with it. Behind her, Sally cried out, just as Bee slammed into Larkwell's shoulder. She planned the collision well: she hit him just hard enough to get his attention and throw him off balance, but not hard enough to knock either of them from their feet. A shout from behind her and pursuing feet. Bee glanced at the reflection in a milliner's window, grinning to see Larkwell running behind her. Months of her new life fitted Bee for darting between shoppers better than Larkwell, and she evaded him without difficulty. But stealing the reticule was never the point. Bee dropped it and slipped into a narrow alley, thinking the chameleon spell-word and hiding behind a pile of crates, careful to quiet her breathing. Around the pile of crates, she could see Larkwell's head silhouetted against the daylight, before he vanished back onto Bond Street. Bee crept out, still hidden by the spell, and peered back the way she'd come. Larkwell, carrying the reticule, jogged back toward Sally and presented it with a slight bow.

"There," she murmured to herself. "Introduction made."

Her two friends continued to talk, and Bee watched them for only another moment before slinking back down the alley and away from Bond Street. She wandered the back streets for a while, wrestling with her feelings. She ought to feel happy, proud to have succeeded in introducing her two friends. And she did. But Bee also felt a twist of jealousy in her gut. She'd been able to ignore it so far, despite seeing so many members of the *ton* every day. They had been faceless strangers living their own, disconnected lives. Seeing Sally and Larkwell, however, drove it home all too clearly what Bee's spring ought to have looked like. She should have been laughing with Sally, well-fed and dressed to the nines, and exploring London on Winston's arm. Instead, she was skulking in alleys, scrounging for castoffs and scraps, indistinguishable from a half-starved preteen boy.

Malorie's harsh words echoed in her mind, as they often did in Bee's darker moods: "Gentlemen prefer wives with curves."

Of course they did. Who wouldn't want a pretty, full-figured girl like Sally? Bee's stomach churned as she thought of Winston, and how he'd looked at her after his first year at university, as if she were water in a desert. She shrugged her shoulders in her shirt that now hung looser than it had. No one could look at her like that now. For the first time, she was glad Winston didn't know where she was. She didn't want him to see her like this. Her heart couldn't bear it.

***

Malorie had no regrets.

She hated to see her husband's grief, but as that grief only proved that his daughter had always held a higher place in his affection than she did, she felt no remorse. She comforted him as only a wife can, ready to fill every void in his heart.

She wore the black crepe and somber face of full mourning like everyone in the house, and no one would have guessed that it was all an act. Only the niggling remains of her doubts about the groom's story marred her peace, and she pushed those aside. She would let nothing ruin this new, Bianca-free life.

CHAPTER 19

***

Winston tried not to count the days, but he couldn't stop himself. Each day was a trial of survival, another four-and-twenty hours that he lived on and Bee did not. The time could be measured in months now, but Winston still saw it as two-and-seventy days, four-and-ninety days, one-hundred-fifteen days. He got out of bed in the morning, dressed, and ate mechanically. He sat in the peony room with his mother. He listened to his father's instructions on the running of the estate. He rode out on Grayling, sticking to the paths around the fields, avoiding the woods.

His life felt hollow, a shell, a series of activities that meant nothing.

A new rumor reached him of a strange creature seen on the other side of the village. It was probably a stray cow seen by a drunk stumbling home from the public house at night. But it woke him up. Winston thought of the fae beast that tore Bee from his life and felt something new: fury. He couldn't let any creature, natural or otherwise, get away with devouring Bianca Snow. It was his duty as her friend to seek vengeance, his duty as the heir to Pinehurst to protect the surrounding area from the predations of supernatural things.

Winston rode out the next day, and for the first time in months, he rode into the woods.

He found nothing, but that didn't stop him from riding out again the next day. It felt good to have a purpose again. He began to reread his notes from university and his journals of spells for any magic that would help him. The book Bee had given him for Christmas contained spells he could use to locate the beast, but they required some trace of it to work from—some piece of it, something belonging to it, its name, anything—the more concrete the trace, the greater the speed and strength of the spell.

So he searched the woods and fields for miles in all directions for any sign of a monster, riding out daily with his eyes peeled for anything out of the ordinary.

***

Bee hadn't anticipated how much London—the wealthier parts, at least—would empty out as the season ended. Parliament finished for the year, so all the lords went home, taking their families to weather the warm months away from the stifling, oven-like town. Bee hadn't been prepared for the heat, either. Summer at Eston Hall had always included the pond, with breezes rustling the leaves and cooling the air. There were no breezes between the tightly packed buildings. Heat settled over the streets and stayed there, unabated. Garbage reeked more than ever; unwashed people did too. Bee knew that she stank of sweat and filth as much as any of them, but there was nothing she could do about it—she had no opportunity to bathe in any kind of privacy, and even if she could wash herself, she had only the one set of clothes.

For the most part, this didn't bother her much. By the time summer set in, she'd been living in a small room with seven younger boys for three months, and she doubted any of them had had a bath in over a year, if ever.

While her nose had adjusted to the scent of unwashed bodies a lot faster than she'd have guessed it would, that didn't prepare her for trying to scrounge through trash in the heat of summer. She couldn't stand it, so she only searched each pile of garbage

CHAPTER 19

for as long as she could hold her breath before moving on. The twins had less to do too. Bond Street was their lay, so with fewer shoppers, there were fewer opportunities for picking pockets. They spent more time wrestling with each other—Bee steadfastly refused to join them—and half the time they came home with nothing at the end of the day.

Jack and Squid were in the same boat as Bee saw when she tagged along with them one day. A few attempts on possible targets but without much luck, and the rest of the time spent wrestling or racing each other. Bee did join the races, but Squid won every time. He was small, light, and fast, and he never let them forget it.

Davy still went out to draw every day, and as there was less to do with the other boys, Bee began tagging along with him sometimes. Davy was always cheerful and friendly, but once he started drawing, he went quiet, as if he'd forgotten that she was there. Each day he drew something different.

Once on the way back to the attic, Bee asked, "How do you decide what to draw each day?"

Davy shrugged. "Whatever's on my mind. Yesterday I drew that dog I saw in the park. I've always wanted one."

"Today you were thinking of St. Paul's Cathedral?"

He shrugged again. "Looks like it'd be cool in there."

Bee thought of how he'd drawn the shade cast by the cathedral building and agreed.

From then on, even on days that she didn't see Davy until they all gathered at night, Bee asked him what he drew that day. He drew some part of the park most often, but sometimes he'd draw a building that he could see from his position on the street. Sometimes it was a dog or a horse. Once it was a boat on the Thames, and another it was his idea of what the ocean would look like. Bee privately marveled that she somehow accumulated artistic friends when she herself could barely draw a straight line.

***

Though Bee knew that there were other gangs of thieves and unwanted children roaming the streets of London, she never had much trouble with them until those summer months. Everyone was frustrated, hot, bored, and restless, which led to bullying. The first time Bee found a couple of surly teens pushing the twins around, she stormed up to the bigger boy and shoved him.

"Leave 'em be," she snarled. She could feel the twins behind her, ready to run or fight, depending on how this went.

"Make me, ye scrawny little git."

Bee scowled at him, sizing him up. The boy couldn't have been more than fourteen, with freckles, unkempt sandy hair, and a cocky smirk. He was taller than she was, but just as malnourished, which meant that he didn't outweigh her by as much as he could have.

"I won't ask again," she said softly. "Leave 'em be."

"And I said 'make me.'"

Without warning, the boy's fist shot toward her, but her lessons with Harry hadn't been for nothing. She'd seen the punch coming, and she dodged aside, darting her own fist into his gut. He doubled over but refused to give up until he'd missed her three more times and she'd laid him out flat. His companion, a scrawny kid still waiting for his growth spurt, inched away down the alley.

"C'mon, mate, they ain't worth it," he said.

CHAPTER 19

"No," Bee agreed, her arms crossed, "they ain't."

The twins, naturally, told the rest of the crew all about the fight that night. Bee sat silent, pretending not to listen. It didn't feel like much of a victory to whoop an untrained boy. All the same, she was proud of herself for defending the twins, and for doing it so efficiently. These boys had given her a home and a family—a loud, rambunctious, uncouth, ill-mannered, disorderly family—when she had nothing and no one. She'd willingly adopted them all as younger brothers, and she'd fight again if they were threatened.

She did get into a few more tussles. Once, Jack was shaken down by a bigger kid while Squid ran for Bee. She arrived just in time to rough up the bully and get Jack's takings back.

Bee had thought that boxing was fun and exciting when she was learning it as a child. Planting a facer on an actual person in an actual fight was a different experience, and she didn't like it. But her stock with the crew rose considerably each time.

***

At last, autumn came, banishing the summer's stuffiness with a foggy chill. Some of London's inhabitants returned from wherever they'd spent the summer sea bathing, and for about a month Bee hoped that the boys would be more successful again. She felt guilty for that hope, as it was based on a life of crime, but in the end she was disappointed. Without the *beau monde* out in force, there just weren't enough wealthy targets. Jack and Squid started begging like Johnny, when they'd given up on their lay for the day, but none of them brought home anything. Bee assumed that whatever little they were given, they ate it then and there. It was too much to ask a growing child with an empty stomach to wait and share.

Somehow, Grim always had something to share at the end of the day. Bee wondered at this, and she noticed how his eyes were extra watchful as the boys divided and devoured the food. All of them were growing, and all of them needed much more sustenance than they were getting. Bee began taking less for herself so the younger ones could have more. She was done growing, after all, and she hated to see them hungry. Bee also began to worry how they were going to get through the winter. She paid attention to whose boots were falling apart the most, whose clothes had the most holes, whose blankets or coats would need to be replaced. What she'd found discarded wasn't enough to keep them all warm.

So she began asking at the churches for charity, and sometimes they gave her a bit of food or an article of clothing. She took her few remaining coins to the Jewish old-clothes traders on Petticoat Lane and bought a pair of not-quite-worn-out boots and a coat with a bit of life left. By the time the first frost came, she'd managed to replace the worst of the boys' rags.

One evening in late October, Grim called Bee over. He was standing by the window, letting down the blanket curtain for the night.

"What's up?" Bee asked softly.

In the dying light that snuck through the gap around the blanket, she could just see his dark eyes glittering in his brown face. In the past seven months, his voice had deepened, and he'd grown an extra few inches so that Bee had to look up at him. "Tomorrow you gotta nick food," he said softly. "I'm running low on blunt, and I have to make it last through winter."

Comprehension dawned on Bee. Grim had stashed away

any excess money from spring so that he could make sure the crew stayed fed throughout the year. He'd never told her much about himself, but she knew that he'd been on the streets for a long time, probably since he was the twins' age or younger. He hadn't been caught off guard by the sudden drop in thieving opportunities.

"There's never quite enough," he went on, glancing back at the others, who were roughhousing, "but they're growing, so we're using it faster."

Bee nodded. "I'm on it."

The next day, Bee put her chameleon spell to work. She didn't dare take much from any one stall, or even from one market. But between what she brought home and what Grim and Davy bought, everyone had something.

Bee had that sick feeling in her stomach again whenever she thought about being a thief, but she couldn't let the boys starve. And she was good at stealing. The markets weren't so different from a busy kitchen, and she was used to moving quickly and quietly. The trick was to make sure she didn't take enough to cause suspicion and to always be well away before the chameleon spell wore off.

Chapter 20

Malorie hesitated for a second outside of Bianca's bedchamber, which had been closed off since the girl's death. The year of mourning was hardly the time to sort through and give away the deceased's possessions, but the room devoted to the little hoyden ate at Malorie like a canker. She could stand it no longer. It had already been nine months, and Christmas was the time for charity. Surely there were needy women who could benefit from the dresses just sitting in Bianca's wardrobe. It wouldn't do to be ungenerous.

Malorie opened the door. The air was stale from being shut up, but otherwise it was as if Bianca had just gone out for the day. Her brush and hand mirror sat on the vanity; a book lay on her nightstand with a ribbon still marking the last page she'd read. A trunk stood beside the wardrobe, and Malorie knew that if she opened it, she'd find it half packed in preparation for a Season in town. She grimaced. The room felt expectant, as if waiting for its owner to return. Well, Bianca wouldn't be coming back.

Standing in front of the large vanity mirror, Malorie surveyed the room and its reflection. What had she expected, coming in here? The servants would be the ones bundling up the clothing to give to the church. There was nothing for

CHAPTER 20

Malorie to do but tell Mrs. Portman to get started. Once everything had been cleared out, Malorie could finally rest, with every trace of Miss Bianca Snow erased from the house.

A spell came to mind as Malorie looked in the mirror, and, idly, she said it. It was a relatively useless spell, though her mother had once used it to great effect, catching Malorie and her sister in an illicit visit to Vauxhall Gardens during her first Season. When cast on a mirror, it would show the owner, wherever they were. This was Bianca's mirror, so it should show Bianca. Of course, the spell would show nothing if the owner was dead, so using it now was a waste of time and magic.

Except that it wasn't. An image spread across the glass, as clear as if it were a window into another place. A gaunt boy with the dark hair and eyes of the Snow family was running, dodging slushy puddles as he darted through the streets. For a brief moment, Malorie felt a sick sense of betrayal, because this was obviously Eston's son by an unknown mistress. But the truth hit her with blunt force as the image began to fade: this was Bianca, the little hoyden herself, in disguise. She was alive, scampering about a city somewhere, wild and untamed as ever.

Malorie's gaze remained fixed on the mirror, even as the bedchamber's reversed image replaced the dirty back streets. Her own reflection stared back at her, pale with horror.

Bianca Snow was alive.

Malorie's fists slowly clenched. She'd known it was too good to be true. The coincidence of the girl's convenient death was too uncanny. The groom had lied. And, like a fool, she'd been taken in because she'd wanted to believe it.

Turning on her heel, she stormed from the room. The groom knew something. She needed to question him. Now. And then he must be silenced.

***

Winston had been riding out in search of the beast every day for months, and still he had found nothing. His father had suggested that perhaps it was time to stop the hunt—the creature must not be in the area any longer—but Winston couldn't. Not yet. There was something he was missing, something important. He couldn't give up on justice for Bee. He couldn't go back to moping around the house. At least his fruitless searching gave him something active to do.

Christmas had passed, the first Christmas without Bee, and her nineteenth birthday, with no one to celebrate it. Snow had fallen in light flurries, but nothing had remained on the ground. Winston rode through the familiar woods, bundled in coat and scarf. His mind wandered back to last Christmas, when Bee was there, and she'd agreed to save him space on her dance card when they were in town together. And to the Christmas before, when she'd gently pressed a frozen handkerchief to his bruised face.

Winston was so lost in his memories that he almost missed the dark shape crumpled at the foot of a tree. His heart surged with hope that he'd finally found the clue he'd been missing. He rode closer, dismounting when he saw that the form was a person. The man's head lifted, and Harry's pained gaze met his. Winston's heart plummeted, taking his breath away. He hadn't seen Harry since Bee's death, hadn't been able to face the groom who had found her remains. Now, he was appalled to see the former prizefighter crumpled in a heap with a dark stain on his coat that looked frighteningly like blood.

CHAPTER 20

Harry's hand shook as he reached out, and Winston dropped to his knees by the man's side, taking the icy hand in his own.

"What happened?" Winston asked. "We need to get you to the house—I'll go for help."

"Too late." Harry's grip was still strong, and he held Winston in place. "She sent a man to kill her. She's going to try again. She *knows*. You have to find Miss Snow before *she* does."

"Who?" Winston demanded. "Bee's dead—who would try to kill her?"

Harry gave his head the tiniest shake. "I lied."

"You—lied? Wait, Bee's *alive*?"

A tiny nod.

"Diamond never spooked," Winston whispered. He'd known it was a story, the same story Bee used every time. He'd known from the start. "But Bee…" would never run away without telling him.

"I'm sorry," Harry said again. "I did… what I had to… to keep her safe." His breath came in shallow gasps.

"What do you mean? Safe from what—from who?" Winston's pulse was racing. Too much was changing too suddenly. His head spun. "Who would want to hurt…" But it was obvious. Harry solemnly held his gaze, nodding slightly as Winston whispered, "Lady Eston?"

"You have to find her." Harry's grip on his hand tightened. "Save our girl."

"I have to save you first."

Winston moved to help the groom to his feet, ready to haul him over Grayling's withers and carry him to Pinehurst, which was the closest house. But Harry shook his head. His breathing was even more labored now, and he was shivering uncontrollably. Even as Winston watched, the older man's head fell back, and he gave a last, shuddering breath.

Winston sat frozen, stunned. Any one piece of the last five minutes was enough to shake his world. Bee was alive. Her stepmother had tried—and was likely going to try again—to kill her. Harry, who had been a teacher and friend to Winston and Bee as much as a groom, had died before his eyes.

Stumbling to his feet, Winston cast up his accounts around the back side of the tree. He wiped his mouth on his sleeve, closed his eyes, and took a deep breath. He had to think.

If Lady Eston was behind Harry's death, then Winston couldn't bring the man back to Eston Hall, or even to the village. Lady Eston would suspect that Winston knew something, and he and his parents would be in danger before he'd even had a chance to look for Bee.

But he couldn't leave Harry here either. Mounting swiftly, he said, "I'll send someone back for you," though he knew the man couldn't hear him, and rode for home.

Winston shut himself in his room for the rest of the day, buried in his books. If he was going to find Bee, he'd have to do it quickly and do it right.

***

Just before Christmas, Johnny spent a night tossing and turning, waking the twins with his fussing. When Bee got up to see what the problem was, and if it could be solved by telling the little boy a story, the grumbling twins rolled the restless child in her direction. Bee laid a hand on Johnny's shoulder, her breath catching as she felt the waves of heat radiating off him. A touch to his forehead confirmed it: he was burning up. Bee whispered the spell-word for fever, grateful for her impeccable memory since she hadn't ever used the spell and had only heard it repeatedly when she'd been ill three years ago. Within minutes, Johnny's temperature dropped and his activity settled. Bee tucked him in beside her, where she'd be the first to know when the spell wore off and his fever climbed again.

When the others left in the morning, Bee and Johnny stayed behind.

"I wanna go out," he whined. "Nuffin wrong with me."

"You're sick," Bee said gently. "Can't be out in the cold with a fever."

"Ain't got a fever."

Bee sighed. "Magic is makin' you feel like you don't. How 'bout I tell you a story?"

Johnny grumbled some more, but he curled up beside Bee where she sat leaning against the wall. She told him one of the *Arabian Nights'* tales, one he hadn't heard yet, and then another that had become one of his favorites. By the end of the third story, her mouth was dry, but Johnny had dozed off with his head pillowed on her thigh. Bee smiled and leaned her head back, allowing herself to doze off for a bit after the interrupted night.

When Grim, Jack, and Squid returned, Bee cast the fever-reducing spell once more before leaving Johnny in their care and jogging to the nearest market. She cast the chameleon spell and was jogging home with an armful of food within minutes.

The next morning, the twins didn't wake as easily as usual. One touch showed that they had caught the fever as well. Bee cast spells on them too, and again on Johnny, whose fever hadn't yet broken. The four of them spent the day shooting dice, telling stories, and napping. Bee made sure that each of them drank several glasses of water, magically filling the jar with water from Eston Hall's spring as often as she needed to. She was relieved when Squid returned with a loaf of bread he'd stolen and Davy had gotten an extra coin or two for his drawing that day—a dragon fighting St. George—which meant that she wouldn't need to go out to the market. She didn't know if she could manage the chameleon spell on top of all the others.

Bee could tell when the boys started feeling better. The twins began wrestling more, and Johnny napped less. She breathed easier; she'd gotten them through it. But she felt worn down herself. She'd slept as much as she could, but magic used energy, just like any exertion, drawing on food as well as sleep. And food was in short supply while she was homebound.

With the boys feeling better now, Bee was able to recover a bit, risking taking a bit more from the markets to make up for what she and the former invalids hadn't eaten.

But then, not a week later, Jack began coughing, and every one of the boys seemed to take a turn with it. Grim refused to stay home. He'd let her spell him in the morning and evening, but he went out in spite of her advice. Squid and the twins recovered quickly and were back out within a few days. But Jack took a long time to recover, continuing to cough even after the others were better. Bee wondered if he had some lung condition that made him more susceptible. There was no money for a doctor, however, so Bee just had to keep on top of the cough suppressing spells.

For nearly a week, Bee and Jack were in the attic alone during the day. Jack paced like a caged animal.

CHAPTER 20

"Can't I go out yet, Whites?" he demanded. "You didn't make Grim stay at all."

"Like I could *make* Grim do nothin'," Bee retorted. "He's older, an' 'e wasn't as sick as you. The cold air ain't good for your lungs when you have a cough."

Jack rolled his gray eyes and ran his hands through his sandy hair. "But I'm *bored*."

Bee sighed. The boy was only seven; of course he was bored cooped up in a single room. "Would you like a story? Dice?"

Jack made a face. "Those are for bantlings and old men."

"What, then?"

"Teach me magic."

Bee stared at him, surprised at how his gray eyes lit up with enthusiasm at the thought. She hated to disappoint him yet again. "Sorry, mate, but no magic while you're sick. Uses energy you need for healing."

His face fell.

"I'll teach you in spring or summer, when no one's sick and we 'ave time to practice."

His eyes lit up with hope again. "Aye? No gammon?"

"No gammon," Bee agreed.

Jack paced the room again, then shot her another bright look. "Teach me to fight?"

"Me?"

"Grim ain't here enough to teach me, and he says I ain't big enough. But you laid a cull low with one dart. Teach me that."

Bee wanted to say no, that it was too much exertion for a sick child, but she couldn't. Not when she'd coerced Winston into teaching her to box when she was only a bit older than Jack. Not when Harry had given her actual lessons, despite what was proper.

She sighed. "I'll teach you some, but only if you promise to rest when I say so."

"Deal."

So Bee began to show Jack how to throw a punch. Jabs, hooks, uppercuts, where the real power came from, how to think like a fighter. She wrapped her hand in an old shirt good only for scraps and held it up as a target. She remembered Harry doing the same for her, and she wondered if he felt the same sense of pride as he watched her learn as she felt watching Jack. Jack's eyes sparked with ferocity as he punched her padded hand, and he bit his lip in solemn concentration as she corrected his form. She realized, watching him, that he was a quick learner, sharper and cleverer than she'd given him credit for. He probably *would* be good at magic, when he got a chance to learn.

At the first sign of fatigue or cough, Bee stopped the lesson and insisted that they rest a while before trying again. The day passed faster and with less complaining than she had expected, and the next day was even better. With only one patient, Bee was able to spare time and magic to slip out and acquire food. It wasn't enough—it was never enough—but she'd do everything in her power, magical and otherwise, to get them through the winter.

Chapter 21

Winston fell asleep at his desk with his head on an open spell book in the early morning hours. Ever since arriving home and dispatching a servant to find Harry's body and take it to the church, he'd been looking through book after book for the spells he'd need. It seemed fitting to his tired brain that the book that contained spells of location was the one Bee had given to him. And the spells he'd learned in his course on defensive magic at Oxford were all written, tiny and precise, in one of the pocket-sized notebooks she'd made.

Blinking awake as the rising sun streamed through his window, Winston stretched and yawned, rubbing a hand over his sticky mouth and rough jaw. He hated sleeping in a chair like that. But the books strewn across the desk reminded him of why he was there and spurred him to get up. He washed his face and changed his clothes, pausing several times through the process to add books to a stack on the chair where he'd been sleeping. Those books would come with him.

Before going down to breakfast, he rang for his father's valet. He'd never wanted or needed one of his own, content to borrow Percy or make do without. Today, he directed the man to pack clothing for a brief trip.

"I'll be gone about a week," Winston said, guessing. He had no idea how long it would take him to find Bee, but he intended to travel light. "Those books on the chair need to be packed as well. Also, have someone deliver this to the housekeeper at Eston Hall and wait for the response. It's urgent."

He handed the valet the note he'd hastily scribbled while waiting for the man. He'd realized sometime in his frantic study last night that the spells he needed required two magicians. The first person who came to mind, who loved Bee and could be trusted to keep her secrets, was Miss Hilton. The governess had left Eston Hall within the week after Bee's funeral, but he hoped Mrs. Portman would have a forwarding address. If not, he'd track down one of his mates from Oxford, preferably Dewey, to help him with the spell.

Winston detoured on his way to the breakfast room, ducking quickly into the peony room and removing Bee's gloves from the filigree box on his mother's desk. He was glad his mother was sentimental, and he swore to himself to never mock her for it. Tucking the gloves into his pocket, he went to join his parents for breakfast.

"You've emerged at last," his mother greeted him with a smile from the foot of the breakfast table. "Did you forget dinner altogether?"

"I would have, if you hadn't been so kind as to send up a tray." He kissed her cheek. "I've been looking over my magic books, and I think it's time to start looking for a job. I'm leaving for town this afternoon."

He held his breath and nonchalantly filled his plate at the sideboard as he waited for their reactions. Lying was Bee's skill, not his. But he couldn't tell his parents the truth, not if it might put their lives at risk. He had no idea how powerful or

CHAPTER 21

vindictive Lady Eston would be, but he loved his parents too much to drag them into this.

"About time," his father said after a stunned silence. "I've been saying for months you ought to stop brooding and distract yourself with work."

He had indeed, and Winston had long since grown tired of hearing it. But it had provided him the perfect excuse, one his parents would willingly believe.

"But must you leave so soon?" His mother frowned. "You aren't even waiting for the Season to start."

"Social engagements have nothing to do with magician's work," his father argued. "If he was intending to host balls and dinner parties, I'd say he ought to wait too, but that's not what he's about."

"No," Winston agreed, "I'm not."

Mother studied him for a moment. He met her eyes, carefully keeping his face impassive. "You've made up your mind, haven't you?"

"I have, Mother."

She sighed. "Very well, then. Write me often, and we'll see you at the very start of the Season."

Winston's cases were packed by the time he'd finished eating, and to his relief, a servant had returned from Eston Hall with an address written on a scrap of paper. He directed that his cases be loaded into his curricle—it wasn't the most practical vehicle for winter, but it was faster than the heavier chaise, and the roads were hard and clear of snow. By noon he was driving away from Pinehurst. He didn't know where he'd end up, but he did know that he had a stop in Potsmouth Hill.

Potsmouth Hill was a village along the road to London. He'd passed through it dozens of times without paying it any mind.

It was like any other country village, a handful of houses and shops clustered around the road, surrounded by farmland. He drove through the village, past the church, then made a right onto a narrow dirt road.

He drew to a stop outside a small, cozy brick cottage with a thatched roof. Winterized gardens stretched between the road and the house. Winston climbed down from the curricle and walked up the path. He'd never given much thought to where servants went when they left, but he was glad Miss Hilton had such a comfortable-looking home to go to. He knocked at the door, and after a brief commotion, a woman in her forties pulled it open. A girl of about five clung to her skirts, staring at Winston with wide eyes. Her mother's gaze scanned him head to toe before she raised an eyebrow.

"Can I help you, my lord?"

"Forgive the intrusion, ma'am, but is this where Miss Hilton lives?"

"Aye, she's my aunt."

"May I see her, please? My name is Winston Graham. She'll remember me."

"Come in, then." She held open the door and gestured him into the room directly to the left, a small parlor with a braided rug on the wood floor and whitewashed walls. The furniture was all of wood with hand sewn cushions on the seats. "I'll let her know you're here." The woman left and closed the door behind her.

A few minutes later, Bee's old governess entered the room. She was just as petite as he remembered, and just as gray—gray hair, gray eyes, gray dress. They shook hands, and she gestured to the chairs before taking a seat herself. He lowered himself to the edge of a chair nearby.

CHAPTER 21

"What brings you here, Mr. Graham?"

Her expression was kind and full of interest, but she wasn't smiling. Winston wondered if she'd lost her reason to smile when Bee disappeared just like he had.

"It's…" Winston searched for words. There was too much to explain, and so much risk in asking for help. But to save Bee, he had no choice. "There's a spell I need another magician's help with, and you were the best person I could think of. Can I… Can I trust you to keep this entirely confidential and not breathe a word to anyone about it?"

Miss Hilton's brow furrowed. "This is quite irregular, Mr. Graham. What spell could you possibly—"

"It's about Bee," Winston interrupted.

Miss Hilton gasped. After the first moment of shock, her spine stiffened and her gaze grew steely. "Explain. You have my promise of confidentiality, but I will not agree to help you until I've heard your whole story. And I won't take part in any necromantic spells or the like."

Now it was Winston's turn to recoil. "No, no, nothing like that. It's not immoral or illegal."

"Then why the secrecy?"

Winston took a slow breath. "Because Bee's alive somewhere, and she's in danger."

Miss Hilton went white. "Tell me everything," she whispered.

"I need another magician to help with the locating spell," he said, after explaining what he knew from Harry of Lady Eston's attempted crimes.

"How does the spell go?" Miss Hilton sat forward, the steel in her eyes and spine intensifying as he'd been speaking. "No time to waste."

Winston hurried back out to the curricle to gather a few

supplies. Together they spread everything out on the floor: a map of England, Bee's gloves, the spell book. Winston flipped the book open to the necessary page. He picked up Bee's gloves in one hand and knelt beside the map, holding the gloves over it. Together, they read the words of the spell. Nothing seemed to happen, but as Winston moved his hand back and forth over the map, he felt heat radiating up from one area. London.

He sat back on his heels and let out a chuckle. This morning's lie wasn't so very false: he would be going to town after all.

"I'll need to get a local map once I get to London and do the spell again for a more precise location," he said, folding the map and gathering everything back up.

"You're going there directly?" Miss Hilton asked.

Winston nodded.

"If you can give me an hour to pack, I'll go too."

Winston blinked at her. She was already bustling around the room, collecting a book and a workbag from beside the chair nearest the hearth. She was halfway out the door to the rest of the house by the time he found his voice. "You want to come?"

"Of course I do, Mr. Graham. You need a second magician."

"I can ask a friend in town—"

"Don't be daft. Another magician could help you locate her, but we don't know if she has a companion or chaperone. *She* may need me more than you do."

He couldn't argue that. What happened after finding Bee hadn't really crossed his mind. He just knew he needed to find her before Lady Eston did. But he couldn't, with propriety, take her to his parents' town house while his mother wasn't there.

Miss Hilton was ready in less than an hour. She found

CHAPTER 21

Winston pacing in the drawing room and let him carry her case out to the curricle. He immediately regretted his choice of carriage, but she told him not to mind.

"I have a warm coat and a strong constitution. And you've brought a blanket. We'll manage."

So with Bee's old governess in the curricle beside him and the cold wind in his face, Winston drove to town.

***

She was in town. Unfortunately for Malorie, Bianca had chosen the rabbits' warren of London in which to hide.

So many side streets, alleys, and crumbling tenements. Too many places to look, too many ways to escape. If only there were a spell that would track her exactly, show Malorie exactly which building, which floor, which room the girl was in, instead of requiring a search of the entire block.

It was better than nothing, Malorie supposed. She'd convinced Eston to come to town early with her—it was only just February, and the *beau monde* wouldn't return in force until after Easter—claiming that she needed new gowns before she could show her face in public. The mourning gowns she'd worn in the country were not fit for the *ton*, and she had nothing in the subdued tones of half mourning to wear when the first year after Bianca's "death" was over.

But she did not spend all day with the modiste and the milliner. She spent it searching this poor, dreary part of town for the girl who should have died last spring.

After two weeks with no success, not even a glimpse of anyone who looked like Bianca in passing, Malorie came up with a new plan. There was a market in the area, one that

Bianca must visit, unless she wanted to walk twice as far. And as the girl could have no access to her father's money and no way to earn her own, she must subsist on stolen food. Malorie knew that Bianca had been taking food from the kitchen for years; one of her magically loyal kitchen maids had leaked the information. She began to talk to the shopkeepers when she went out. She learned that petty theft was common—and the shopkeepers were all too eager to complain to a listening ear. One round woman with crooked teeth who ran a vegetable stall was particularly talkative, and Malorie took the opportunity while the woman's mouth ran on to silently cast the spell of loyalty. It had the unfortunate side effect of making the woman talk more, but it also led to her agreeing to help the viscountess catch a particular thief. Malorie gave no details, and she stayed home the next day to prepare.

She took an apple—somewhat shriveled now after months in the cellar—and set it on her dressing table. With the door to her bedchamber locked, she recalled the spells that a magician had given her mother to help her father when he was ill. One spell would mimic the soporific and pain reducing effects of laudanum, provided only a small bite was taken, but in a larger dose—like eating the whole apple—the result would be fatal. Another spell slowed the heart rate, which also ought to be ingested only in small quantities. A third spell strengthened the other two, to make all effects last longer. The final spell was a bit of her aunt's not-quite-black magic, making the apple appealing only to Bianca Snow and repellant to anyone else.

It wasn't the most foolproof plan, Malorie admitted to herself, as she brought the apple to the market the next morning. But one must make the best of the hand one was dealt.

CHAPTER 21

The shopkeeper took the fruit cheerfully, placing it beside her own basket of slightly withered apples, as if it had merely fallen from the pile and been forgotten—the perfect place for an opportunistic thief to grab it when no one was looking. She chatted for a few minutes, and Malorie gritted her teeth and clenched her fists with impatience. Soon she need have nothing to do with this low-bred chatterbox, but she couldn't let rudeness taint the loyalty spell, nor could she let the woman figure out how serious the magic on the apple really was.

At last, there was a pause as the woman drew breath, and Malorie jumped in to thank her effusively and remind her to send word as soon as the apple was taken.

"Of course, your ladyship, anything for you." The woman curtsied clumsily. "We'll find the missing child and get 'em right back to you."

Malorie forced a smile before walking away. If all went well, no one would ever see Bianca again.

Chapter 22

Once Jack was feeling better from the cough, another round of fevers went through the crew. January passed for Bee in a blur of spells, cool wet cloths, and stories. She didn't remember the last time she'd left the attic room. Grim looked grimmer than ever as he brought home less and less each evening. Even Davy's energy and optimism had faded. He was back on his feet after his own fever had broken, but Bee could see that fatigue still plagued him. Bee herself was run off her feet with exhaustion. She napped as often as she could and limited extra spells.

By the time everyone was over the last wave of illness, February was well underway. Bee felt weak with relief when she swung herself out of the attic window and dropped down the stairs. The streets may not be lovely, and the air may not be fresh, but any change from the closed up attic room was welcome. The boys had all scattered in their usual directions, none of them waiting for her. They'd gotten used to leaving her behind to deal with the sick ones, and no one thought twice about it. Not that Bee minded. She'd been enclosed in a room with little boys for most of the winter without a break; she could use a day to herself.

She took her time going to the markets. There were three

CHAPTER 22

she usually visited when she could, and she went to the farthest first. Her stomach ached with emptiness, and her head felt weak, so instead of only grabbing things that would be good for sharing, she also snagged a hot cross bun from the baker's stall. She ate this herself as soon as she was a block away from the market, forcing herself to eat it slowly and chew before swallowing. It didn't erase the ache, but it helped a bit.

By the time she'd finished at the second market, she'd filled her small satchel with cheese and bread and pasties. She'd found the satchel in the fall, just after she started thieving for real, and she wore it slung across her body under her buttoned coat. Now if she could just grab a couple more things to fill her coat pockets, she'd have enough for all eight of them to eat tonight.

She surveyed the final market from a shadowed alley. This was the market she'd stolen from most often this winter. She hadn't had time to go farther. She needed to be extra careful here and not take much.

A stall holding hothouse fruits and vegetables caught her eye. She hadn't had a single piece of fruit all winter. Suddenly, a stab of homesickness stole her breath. She missed the days of canning at the end of summer when Mrs. Cole stored away fruits for winter; missed the hothouses at Eston Hall that provided strawberries and lemons all year; even missed the root vegetables from the cellar that they ate until the first plantings of spring came up.

What she wouldn't give right now for a single bite of a juicy pear.

Bee cast the chameleon spell for the third time that day and crept closer to the stall. The pull of fresh produce was too strong to fight. Her body craved it like air or water. An apple that had fallen from the basket caught her eye. It was the wrong season for apples, even with hothouses, and most of these were wrinkled from months in the cellar. But this fallen one was less spotted, less shriveled. It still looked juicy. Bee couldn't help imagining the crisp crunch as her teeth bit through it. She nearly swooned as her mouth watered. Without another moment's thought, she grabbed it and slipped away from the market. Halfway home, she stopped. She'd share it with the boys, of course—they hadn't eaten fruit any more recently than she had—but she couldn't bear to wait another minute for her own piece. The little folding knife she'd taken to carrying was out of her pocket in a flash, a slice cut and in her mouth before she'd even consciously chosen to do it.

Bee groaned with pleasure. The apple crunched as she chewed, the juice coating her mouth with sweet bliss. She cut another thin sliver and ate it slowly, savoring each nibble. With a sigh, she pocketed the apple and the knife. She loved her adopted brothers too much to keep it all to herself. Forcing the apple from her mind, she started again for home.

At the foot of the stairs, she started feeling a bit strange, like her head was disconnected from her body and floating above. She blinked, coming back to herself. The little she'd eaten today must have made her body realize just how badly she needed food. She'd get up to the attic, eat with the boys, and be fine.

She felt even stranger by the time she pulled herself through the window, tired and weak and slow. She removed her coat and unslung the full satchel. The twins and Grim were already back, and the younger boys cheered at the sight of the full bag. Grim watched her with a frown.

"You done in, Whites?" he asked. "You don't look right."

CHAPTER 22

"I'm fine," Bee said, shrugging her coat back on and reaching out for the low angled roof to steady herself. "Just a bit off. I 'aven't been out much lately. Maybe went too far." She sat where she stood, feeling suddenly faint.

The twins dropped the satchel and came over to stare at her too. "You eat today?" one asked. The other gave a sharp nod and added, "Anything that tasted funny?"

Bee shook her head. Nothing had tasted funny at all, only delicious. "A bun this morning, and then the apple." She managed to extract the apple from her pocket and tossed it to Grim. He held it gingerly in his big hand, his dark eyes darting from the fruit to her.

Sitting up felt like too much effort for Bee, and she lay back on the floor. "Need to kip," she mumbled. "Wake me to eat."

She heard the mutters from the boys but didn't listen. She felt too heavy all over.

"Poison?"

"Gotta be. Apple ain't right. Don't let anybody eat it."

"What do we do? Whites is the one who'd know magic to help, and 'e's…"

Bee's mind drifted off, her consciousness fading to black.

Chapter 23

Winston stalked the streets of London, feeling more and more helpless. It had been a fortnight since he and Miss Hilton had surprised the housekeeper of his parents' town house by showing up unexpectedly. Repeating the locating spell over a map of London had shown him the general neighborhood, leaving him to do a lot of footwork. He'd asked everyone he crossed paths with if they'd seen a girl of Bee's description, but no one had. He'd knocked on doors, greased palms, done everything he could to get information, but there was none to be had. For the past few days he'd taken to simply walking the streets, praying that he'd run across her.

Nothing.

He'd turned his steps toward home as the afternoon wore on, eventually leaving the decrepit buildings and cramped streets behind for the more open lightness of Mayfair. He passed a park, one that he'd played in as a child, one that he'd intended to walk through with Bee during her debut Season. But she wouldn't be there. The map had shown quite clearly—even when he cast the spell again a week into the search in the hopes that he'd get a clearer answer—that Bee was several blocks away from the part of town she'd been born to.

CHAPTER 23

A boy crouched on the side of the street, drawing with charcoal on the flagstones. Winston stepped aside to walk around the picture, glancing down only with mild curiosity as he passed. He froze mid-step, his heart stopping cold only to begin racing like a spooked horse.

"Who is that?" His voice was carefully blank, devoid of emotion.

The boy looked up from his drawing, his longish brown hair falling over his eyes. He gave his head a shake to toss the hair back. "What's it to you?"

Winston's gaze was locked on the black and gray drawing. Even without color, even on the rough street, he knew that face. It was thinner than he remembered, but it was her. The boy had the makings of an artistic genius: he'd captured the spark in Bee's eyes, the fierce determination in her set jaw. Her hair was short, about the same length as the boy's, actually, but there was no question of who it was.

Winston stared at the image in silence for a moment, then said, "It reminds me of someone I used to know, and whom I very badly miss. Who is it?"

"My brother." The boy frowned at the picture. Winston cut him a glance and raised his eyebrows. The boy shrugged. "We ain't blood."

Winston nodded. Bits of the puzzle were falling into place. No wonder no one had recognized his description of Bianca, the girl—she'd been disguised as a boy all this time. He studied the picture again, and when he glanced at the boy, the little artist was also examining it, but with a sad look in his eyes.

"What—what happened to him?" Winston nearly choked on the words, but there was something in the boy's expression that forced the question.

The boy scowled up at him for a moment, then dropped his gaze and sighed. "Poison. Magic. Dunno. 'E won't wake up."

Winston's chest went tight. "Will you take me to him?"

The boy glared at him. "Not takin' a toff anywhere near, 'less you're gonna pay a magician to help."

"I am a magician."

The boy's eyes widened, and he got to his feet. "A proper one, trained an' all?"

Winston nodded. "Educated at Oxford."

"How much?"

"Pardon?"

"How much you chargin'? Ain't got more'n a penny or two."

Winston shook his head. "No charge. Like I said, your—brother—reminds me of someone. I'll do what I can if you'll take me to him."

The boy nodded and picked up his charcoal and his hat, slipping the single coin into his shirt. "C'mon, then. I'm Davy. Who're you?"

"Winston Graham." Winston followed the boy back in the direction that he'd come, away from Mayfair.

Davy dodged his way through traffic, both foot and vehicular, without breaking his pace. Winston jogged to keep up, offering hurried apologies whenever he bumped into someone because his eyes were on his guide. The boy looked back at him a few times to make sure he was still coming, but it was clear from his rushed pace that urgency had mixed with a bit of hope, and he was impatient. Winston was impatient too, and they were back in the neighborhood he'd walked through earlier that afternoon in less than half the time it had taken him to leave it.

Davy led him down an alley and around the back of one

of the leaning tenements. The boy scampered up the stairs, hoisting himself up and through an attic window as if it was nothing. Winston hadn't done any kind of acrobatics in years, not since climbing trees with Bee as a child, but he managed to haul himself up and in. He fell gracelessly to the wooden floor and got to his feet, dusting himself off before looking around.

Seven gaunt, dirty boys stared at him with wide, distrustful eyes. The youngest was barely as tall as Winston's waist, and the others ranged in size and age. The oldest was in his teens, almost a man, with the shadow of his first straggly beard on his brown chin. His dark eyes were the sharpest, and he shot Davy a glare.

"Who's this?" he demanded.

"Magician," Davy said eagerly. "Saw a picture I drew of Whites, said 'e reminded him of someone. Said 'e'd come for free."

The oldest boy turned that sharp glare on Winston. "You know Whites?"

"Not by that name," Winston said. "But whether he's the person I know or not, I'm here to help."

The smaller boys shuffled aside as the oldest strode past, over to one side of the tiny attic where a figure lay wrapped in an overcoat. Winston followed, magically igniting a rushlight that sat nearby. In the flickering light, he took in the face of the sleeping figure.

It was Bee. Without question. Her eyes were closed and her breathing slow. She looked as gaunt and haggard as the boys that crowded in behind him. Her raven hair was unwashed, her pink cheeks streaked with soot and dirt. Still, she was the most beautiful thing he'd ever seen.

It took a moment for him to find words and the breath to

say them. "What happened?"

"This apple." The oldest boy knelt on Bee's other side and pulled a shriveled piece of fruit from the pocket of her coat. He handed it to Winston. "Dunno where 'e got it, but 'e collapsed soon as 'e got in."

"How long ago?"

"Four days. We tried givin' 'im water, but 'e couldn't swallow it."

Winston dropped to his knees beside Bee, trying to hide his dismay. She was already skin and bones, and then to go four days without food or water? Her chest rose and fell as she breathed, but the movement was so slight, so slow, that he was certain she had only hours to live if he didn't wake her now.

"Give me space." His voice came out hoarse, and he swallowed. "I need water, too. Have you a cup?"

A boy with red hair and freckles hurried up with a chipped cup and a larger jar. "Whites used to fill it for us with magic, but it's been empty since…"

Winston nodded and thought the spell-word to fill the cup. A ripple of surprise passed through the boys, who had backed away a few feet but still hovered, watching. Winston poured water into the palm of his right hand. He set the cup down and picked up the apple with his left, muttering the spell as he trickled the palmful of water over it. The water sizzled and hissed, sending up an acrid vapor. Winston waved it away, looking at the apple with increased alarm. Bee was lucky she was only passed out on the floor for days. If she'd eaten more than the slice she'd cut, she would have been dead four days ago.

Sick tension filled Winston as he set down the apple and turned to Bee. He didn't have a proper spell for this. The fruit had been filled with a jumble of magic that all played on each other to lethal effect. He'd have to make do with basic spells of healing, something to help her body reject the toxic spells, to cleanse her of their residue. He laid a hand on her forehead, noticing against his will just how soft her skin still was. He cast two spells like that, then he took another palmful of water and cast a spell onto it before gently prying open her mouth and trickling the water in. The last spell was one he'd never thought to use. It was a general come-back-to-us spell, used only on the most dire cases, but it had to be administered a very specific way. Winston bent over and lowered his mouth to Bee's, murmuring the spell-word against her dry, cracked lips. Then, though it wasn't precisely part of the spell, he pressed his lips to hers in a gentle kiss, praying with all he had. She had to wake. He couldn't lose her again. He couldn't survive her dying a second time.

He sat back and looked across Bee's body at the oldest boy. The boy's face had become a hard, expressionless mask, and his eyes burned as he glared at Winston. Before Winston could wonder about this, a small hand jerked him backward by the shoulder. He half toppled, stumbling to his feet just in time for a fist to slam into his stomach. Winston caught his small assailant's fist in his as it swung for him again, and he met the furious gray eyes of a sandy-haired boy who looked too livid for words.

Winston couldn't figure out why the boy was so angry, so he tried distraction. "Where'd you learn to throw a punch like that?"

"Whites taught me," the boy snarled.

"'Whites' and I learned from the same teacher," Winston said coolly, releasing his grip on the boy's fist. "So I suggest you lay off."

"Lay off? You ain't go no right!"

Winston dodged another left hook, realizing suddenly what the final spell must have looked like to the boys. They didn't know anything about the magic, what it was for or how it must be cast. They didn't know that Bee was a girl. All they saw was a strange man who was supposed to be healing their friend bend down and kiss the boy. He grimaced. "It was a spell," he explained roughly. "One of several spells I cast to save your friend. If they worked, 'Whites' should be waking up any minute."

Both of them looked over at the prone figure who at that moment began to stir.

Chapter 24

Bee's head ached like someone had attacked her with an axe and a mallet at the same time. Her eyes felt gritty and her throat was dry.

"Bloody 'ell," she croaked, raising one hand to her temple. "What 'appened?"

She blinked up at the seven worried faces hovering over her in the dim light. No—eight. Bee stared at the extra face, blinking the dry blurriness from her vision, because she couldn't possibly be seeing clearly.

"Winston?" she gasped. The sudden intake of air caught on her dry throat, and she coughed. Winston's hand reached out with the chipped cup of water.

"Drink slowly."

She raised herself onto her elbow and accepted the cup, sipping it carefully. Each swallow made her thirstier. She wanted to gulp the whole cup down, and another right after it, so she distracted herself by looking around. She was still in her coat. The boys were all there. The dim light suggested that it was evening. She wondered if Grim had been able to get enough food for them all.

She finished the water, and Winston took the cup from her and refilled it before handing it back. She stared at him while she drank. He looked tired. There were shadows under his eyes that she'd never seen there before.

"What are you doing here?" she whispered.

"Saving your life," he said with a slight quirk to his lips. "I ran across Davy on the street, and he said they needed a magician to save his brother." He raised an eyebrow.

A bit of warmth curled through Bee's heart as she glanced at Davy. She'd been thinking of the boys as her brothers, but she hadn't realized they saw her the same way.

She looked back at Winston. "I can't go back."

"I know," he said simply. "But you can't stay here. She knows where you are."

Bee nodded. The apple had been Malorie's work. As soon as her stepmother discovered that Bee hadn't died—again—there would be another attempt. And the boys would be at risk now too. She couldn't stay and put their lives in danger.

She struggled to a sitting position. "I'll go. Just…" She didn't know what she wanted to say. *Give me a minute to gather myself before I try to stand. Let me say goodbye to the family who took me in when I needed them. Promise me that you'll never let me out of your sight again.* She said none of these.

Johnny knelt beside her, jostling her so that water slopped up the side of the cup. "You're leaving?" His big blue eyes melted her.

"I have to," she said. "Someone's tryin' to do me in. It ain't safe for you if I stay."

"We'll protect you." Jack crossed his arms, shooting a glare at Winston. Bee didn't know why he'd taken a dislike to her magician friend, but she couldn't help smiling at his ferocity.

"Your fists won't be much use," she said. "Mine weren't."

Jack scowled but didn't argue.

CHAPTER 24

After a few more minutes, Bee was on her feet. She and Winston moved toward the window. "Bye," Bee said, looking one more time at the cluster of dirty boys that she loved like brothers. "It won't be forever."

She gave a weak smile to Grim and Davy, who stood a little apart. She'd never been good at reading Grim's expressions, but Davy looked shaken. The events of the evening must have taken a toll on him. Bee wished she could pull them all in for a big hug, but that would ruin everything. Winston had clambered out the window while she said her last goodbye, and now she slipped through the opening as easily as if she'd been doing it all her life. She noticed Winston's hands come up as if to steady her, but he didn't touch her. She wished he would. They descended the stairs silently and walked side by side to the nearest main street. Winston hailed a hack and handed her into the carriage before seating himself across from her.

Bee waited for him to say something as the carriage rolled off, but he continued to watch her, his eyes full of some intense emotion that she couldn't place. She felt exposed and vulnerable for the first time in ages. She could feel every grain of dirt embedded in her skin, every bit of oil in her hair. For the first time in months, she felt improper in her boys' clothes and embarrassed at how they hung loose over her complete lack of feminine curves. She was sitting in the presence of the one person whose opinion she cared about, and he wouldn't look away. Her eyes burned, and she turned to look out the window.

"What is it, Bee? What's wrong?" His voice was so gentle, so heartbreakingly familiar.

She'd promised a long time ago that she'd never lie to him. "I didn't want you to see me like this," she whispered.

"I thought you were *dead*." The words, a startling non sequitur, were as hoarse as if they were ripped from him. "They told me an unnatural monster had eaten the girl I loved—my best friend." Bee turned to him in horror, her heart wrenching at the agony on his face. "And then, when I finally found you again, you genuinely were inches from death's door. I couldn't survive losing you a second time. And you think I care what you're *wearing*?"

Bee gaped at him. She wanted to protest that the clothes were only part of it, but emotion choked her, and a single tear leaked from her eye. Instantly, Winston crossed to sit beside her, pulling her into his arms.

"Honeybee," he murmured.

She sobbed against his chest. Very few actual tears fell—she was too dehydrated for her body to waste water on sadness—but Winston's coat would have been soaked. Just being near him again released the dam of all the times over the years that she'd suppressed the pain and refused to cry.

When her sobs had subsided to shuddery breaths, Winston kissed the top of her head. "Why didn't you come to me? You knew I would have traveled to the ends of the earth with you."

Bee shook her head slightly but didn't raise it from where she rested against him. "Pinehurst was the first place she'd look for me," she said shakily. "And the two of us together—she would have found us within a week. It was safer if you didn't know anything about it." She hiccuped and pressed her eyes shut tight. "I'm sorry I didn't say goodbye."

Winston kissed her hair again and held her tighter, but he didn't say anything. The hack pulled to a stop, and Winston released her as a footman came out from the house to lower the step and open the door. Bee got to her feet, but her head

CHAPTER 24

suddenly swam, and she wobbled. Winston was there to catch her. Instead of helping her climb down, he scooped her up in his strong arms. He let out a low curse.

"Honeybee, there's nothing left of you."

Bee wrapped her arms around his neck and buried her face in his shoulder so that she wouldn't have to see the worry and pain in his eyes. He barked out orders as he entered the house, calling for a bath to be drawn in the guest room and a fire to be lit, and for tea to be sent up. He carried her up the stairs and through a door. Bee raised her head to look around as he set her lightly on a wooden chair. A servant was quickly lighting a fire on the hearth, and by its light, Bee could see that the room was large and elegant. The walls were papered in green and white stripes, and the counterpane on the bed was embroidered in vines of green ivy. The comfortable chairs by the fire were of matching green damask. More servants carried in a large tub that they began to fill. The water steamed, and Bee watched it longingly. She'd never wanted a bath so badly.

An older woman bustled in. "What's going on, Mr. Graham? Have you found her?" Bee looked up at her, startled. Miss Hilton gasped when she saw Bee. "Miss Snow!"

"Miss Hilton? How…"

Tears swam in the woman's eyes, but before she could say or do anything, someone else arrived with a tea tray. Winston reached for the teapot, but Bee said, "Could I just have water, please?"

Winston gave her a look that said he'd give her the world if she asked for it. He filled the teacup with water using the spell she'd used herself so many times. As she sipped it, she noticed what was on the plate.

"Scones," she whispered.

Winston's face lightened for the first time, and he cut one of the scones in half, slathering it with jam and adding a dollop of clotted cream. "Sweet tooth," he teased, handing it to her.

Bee tried to eat it slowly, to savor it, but it was gone in four bites that she didn't remember chewing.

"No more for now," Winston said. "Bathe first, then you can have more. You've gone without food for too long—you'll get sick if you eat too much at once."

Bee knew he was right, but it was an effort to tear her gaze away from the other half of the waiting scone. Miss Hilton distracted her by shooing Winston from the room to find some clean clothes for Bianca. Once he and all the servants had gone, she helped Bee out of her clothes and into the tub. Assisting with her bath wasn't a task for a governess, but Miss Hilton didn't seem to mind. Bee sank into the hot water with a sigh, watching as the older woman bundled up her filthy old clothes with a look of disgust.

"Don't destroy them," Bee said quickly. "Please. Just have them washed. I know… I know some boys who could use them."

Miss Hilton considered her a moment, then nodded and set the bundle outside the door. Then she came over with a bar of soap and began to scrub Bee top to bottom. Bee couldn't remember the last time someone had given her a bath, but she still felt weak and tired, and it was so nice to just let someone care for her.

A knock sounded, and Winston's voice called that he was leaving clean clothes outside the door. Miss Hilton brought them inside, then helped Bee from the water. Bee's fingers and toes had gone wrinkly, and her skin was pink from all the

CHAPTER 24

scrubbing, but it felt so good to be clean. Miss Hilton helped her on with a nightgown and wrapped a dressing gown on top of that. They were both much too loose; Bee guessed they had come from Lady Rowland's dressing room.

Once she was dry and dressed, Miss Hilton settled Bee in one of the chairs by the fire with the other half of the scone and a cup of tea. Bee used to take her tea with plenty of sugar, but having gone without sweetness for so long, the jam was almost too much, and she appreciated the slightly bitter brew.

A maidservant bustled in, pulling back the covers on the bed and putting a brick that had been warming on the hearth between the sheets.

Miss Hilton sat in the chair across from Bee. "I'll be staying in here with you, Miss Snow, at least for tonight. You've had quite a close call, and you need someone to keep an eye on you."

Bee opened her mouth to protest that no one needed to lose sleep over her, but what came out was an enormous yawn. She smiled ruefully, and Miss Hilton's prim expression softened.

When Bee had finished her tea and scone, Miss Hilton shooed her into bed and tucked her beneath the covers. She smoothed the hair off of Bee's face in a rare show of tenderness.

"We've been worried about you, Miss Snow," she said softly.

Bee didn't respond. Her eyes were already drifting shut. The bed was so incredibly comfortable, and she was so warm under the blankets with the fire crackling nearby.

Sometime in the dark of night, Bee startled awake with a cry. She'd dreamed that she was back in the attic room and that all the boys lay motionless, barely breathing, poisoned by the rest of the wretched apple. Bee struggled to get to them, to help them, but she couldn't move—she, too, was bound by magic.

She sat up in bed, gasping for breath, her hand pressed over her heart. A figure moved in the near dark by the banked fire. She let out a whimper.

"Hush, Miss Snow, dear," came Miss Hilton's voice as the woman crossed the room to her. Bee relaxed as she drew close and Bee could make out her face. "Quite a nightmare, I expect. You've been thrashing about for a few minutes now."

"She found me—them—all of us," Bee whispered. "I couldn't move."

Miss Hilton patted her arm. "Rest easy. This house is under more protection spells than Prinny's palace. Nobody can get to you while Mr. Graham and I are here." She smiled. "As long as you're awake, would you like something to eat?"

Bee stared at her, then at the tray waiting on the nearest table. She wasn't used to meals in the middle of the night, even at Eston Hall where she could sneak into the kitchen, but just thinking of food made her hungry. "Yes, please."

There was soft white bread and sharp cheese along with a small gooseberry tart. Bee ate all of it, washing it down with the clear water that she knew had come from Pinehurst's well. Sated, she sank back onto the pillows and fell asleep.

In the morning, Miss Hilton helped Bee dress in another borrowed item from Lady Rowland's closet, a morning dress of deep green with a high neck and long sleeves.

"Mrs. Stephens says that her ladyship always leaves a partial wardrobe here in case she forgets to pack something," Nanny said as she helped Bee with the buttons.

Lady Rowland wasn't a large woman by any means, but the dress dwarfed Bee. Nanny found a ribbon from somewhere and used it as a belt to snug the gown a bit closer at the waist. Bee felt ridiculous, and she couldn't decide if she wished more

CHAPTER 24

for her old dresses from home or for the trousers she'd taken off last night. Wearing gowns again was going to take some getting used to.

Bee soon discovered that as far as Miss Hilton was concerned, she was an invalid to be nursed back to health with the utmost care, just as she had been after her bout of winter fever. She was tucked into a chair by the built-up fire with a lap blanket and breakfast. Not just breakfast—a small meal was brought up every few hours. Bee was never allowed to eat much at a time, but the household seemed determined to get a year's worth of missed food into her as quickly as possible. She appreciated their concern, and she was glad to rest with a book, but she wished Winston would come to see her. She hadn't seen or heard from him since her bath last night, and it was almost harder to bear not being near him now that they were in the same house.

Chapter 25

Winston paced his father's study as he waited for an update from Miss Hilton. He hadn't slept last night, knowing how close to death Bee had come, knowing that she was still in danger. He had to restrain himself from going to her room to check on her—if he was close enough to see her, he wouldn't be able to stop himself from holding her in his arms again. He'd missed her so badly.

Mrs. Stephens poked her head in with a message from the governess. "Miss Snow has eaten two meals this morning and another overnight. She's reading by the fire now. No cause for concern, sir."

Winston thanked her. With that reassurance, he left the house.

He didn't know what time Lord Eston would go to the club, but it was his best hope of catching him. Winston had considered, briefly, sending a note around requesting that Bee's father call at the house, but he was afraid Lord Eston would bring his lady along, and that couldn't happen. And there was no polite way to ask a man to please not bring his wife.

So Winston went to the club to wait. His father had taken him along once or twice, and it had seemed the dullest place to

CHAPTER 25

a teenaged boy—just a bunch of old men smoking, discussing politics, and placing bets on stupid gossip. Winston wasn't much more impressed now, but he took up a position in a leather armchair in the reading room, using a newspaper to hide the fact that his eyes were glued to the door.

He'd been there for nearly an hour when Lord Eston entered. Bee's father was immediately hailed by Lord Ashbury, and Winston waited while the two discussed an upcoming horse race. He was on his feet and crossing the room as soon as Eston excused himself.

"Lord Eston, sir," he called.

Eston turned, a brief flicker of pain flashing across his face before he forced a smile. Winston recognized the pain. He'd avoided their neighbors for the past year for the same reason: seeing them made him think of Bee. But Eston was friendly, saying, "Graham! Good to see you, son. What brings you to town so early?"

"Magician's work," Winston said, truthfully. "But I was hoping to catch you. There's something I'd like you to see at the house. Could you come by?"

"How's tomorrow morning?"

Winston shook his head. "It's rather urgent. Could you come now?"

Eston, bemused, glanced around the front room of the club and shrugged. "If it's that important, I'm at your service."

"Thank you, sir. It is."

They returned to the house, and after inviting Eston to have a seat in the drawing room, Winston quietly sent a footman up to ask Miss Hilton and Bee to come down. He rejoined Bee's father, who looked at him curiously.

"Well? Where is it, son?"

"Someone's bringing it now," Winston said. He paced to the window, unable to sit still. Eston, too, stayed on his feet, moving toward the fireplace to examine the painting over the mantle.

A light knock turned Winston's attention to the door. Bee entered the room, arm in arm with Miss Hilton. Bee was wearing one of his mother's dresses, and not a particularly flattering one, but she was still heart-stoppingly beautiful.

"Winston?" She saw him by the window and smiled. "What—" But at the sound of her voice, her father whirled around, and she noticed him for the first time. "Papa?" she squeaked.

Eston's face went ashen, and he gaped, open-mouthed, for a long, silent moment. At last he breathed, "Snowflake?"

Bee let go of Miss Hilton's arm and rushed toward him. Her father closed the distance between them in three huge steps and gathered her into a tight hug. "You're alive," Eston repeated, over and over. He stepped back and held her at arm's length. Tears streamed down both of their faces. Winston turned back to the window to give them privacy, but he could hear them easily enough.

"Where have you been? What happened? They told me you were dead!"

"It's a long story, Papa. Will you sit?"

"Yes, of course, but—snowflake, we have to tell Malorie! She's been beside herself. She'll be overjoyed—"

"No," Bee said sharply, cutting him off. Winston looked over then to see shock in Eston's eyes. "She wouldn't be happy at all, and no one will say a word to her." There was a firmness to Bee's jaw that hadn't been there before, and a hardness to her expression that brooked no opposition.

Her father faltered. "But, Bianca…"

CHAPTER 25

"Perhaps we should sit and hear Bee's story now." Winston stepped away from the window. "I'm sure it will clear up a lot of questions. There's still so much I don't know. Miss Hilton, will you ring for tea, please?"

So the four of them settled into seats. Bee sat on the loveseat with her father beside her. Winston sat in a chair opposite, with Miss Hilton presiding over the tea things. Eston refused to relinquish Bee's hand, even to eat or drink.

"You were in town already, Papa, when I had to run away."

Bee's tale was short and simple, but she told it like a natural storyteller. She told of Harry taking her aside and helping her to disguise herself and how she'd gone first to her father's house in town but he had already been called back to the country. She told of meeting Davy and joining the boys. Color rose in her cheeks as she admitted to stealing with the aid of magic. She told of the hard winter and doctoring the boys with spells. And she told of finding the apple, and eating those glorious bites, before passing out in the attic room.

Winston watched Eston's face as he listened, emotions racing over it ranging from shock to horror to disgust to confusion. When Bee finished, she looked across at Winston. "How did you come to be there just in time?"

"I, too, met Davy." Bee grinned, and it was irresistible—he had to smile back. "I could not have been more shocked to see the face of the one person I wanted most to find, drawn in lifelike detail in charcoal on stone."

"I don't understand," Lord Eston said. "Was the apple poisoned?"

Winston shook his head. "Spelled. A handful of spells that may not have done much damage on their own, but together…" The memory of Bee's still form and slow breathing brought that horrible tightness back to his chest. "Bee's love for those boys saved her. If she'd eaten the whole apple instead of bringing it back to share, she'd have been dead long before I reached her."

Eston clutched Bee's hand convulsively. "And you think Malorie had something to do with this?"

Bee nodded. "She's hated me for years, Papa."

Eston sighed. "I knew you didn't love each other like I'd hoped, but I never dreamed..." He got to his feet, tugging Bee up with him so he could pull her in for another hug. "I won't say a word to her, I promise. But now there are things I need to do."

Bee nodded into his shoulder. Winston could feel her watching as he followed her father out of the room.

"Can we talk a moment?" he asked, gesturing to the open door of the breakfast room across the hall. They stepped inside, and Winston closed the door behind them.

Eston rubbed a hand over his face. "This is all so much to take in. I will deal with Lady Eston, but it may take some time to gather proof."

"Bee is safe here," Winston said. "We have this house covered top to bottom in protective spells."

"Thank you. Thank you for saving my daughter."

"Sir," Winston hesitated, but he'd waited too long not to ask, "do you remember what we spoke about before I left for university?"

A small smile softened Eston's bleak expression. "You still want to marry her?"

"With all my heart."

"Then you have my blessing. Get a special license and send me a note with the time. I think a small private ceremony

CHAPTER 25

in the safety of this house would be best." He reached out to shake Winston's hand. "I feel better knowing she's under your protection, Graham. I trust you not to let her come to harm."

"Never, sir. Thank you."

Bee's father left. Winston took several slow, deep breaths. His heart was racing, soaring, swooping. Now to ask Bee.

***

Winston seemed agitated when he returned to the drawing room. Bee wondered what her father could have said. She was about to ask when Miss Hilton rose from her chair.

"Mr. Graham, would you mind sitting with Miss Snow a moment? I need to speak with the cook about her dinner." Miss Hilton's smile was enigmatic as she disappeared out the door.

Winston came and sat beside Bee on the couch. She turned to smile up at him and said softly, "Thank you for bringing Papa here." Impulsively, she slid her arms around his waist and squeezed him, her cheek pressed against his collarbone. His arms enfolded her, and his chin rested lightly on her head. Bee loved how she fit so nicely against him, how warm and strong he was, how safe and cared for he made her feel. She didn't want to move again, ever.

"I—I don't think I've thanked you yet for saving my life," she murmured. She lifted her head. "Thank you." Bee trailed off. She had to tip her head way back because he was so tall, but even so, their faces were only a few inches apart. At this distance, the intensity in his eyes was scorching. Slowly, Winston lowered his head until their mouths met. Bee melted. The kiss was soft and sweet and heartfelt.

Winston pulled back to look her in the eyes again. "Will you marry me, Honeybee?"

Bee nodded, not trusting her voice. She swallowed hard. "Did Papa...?"

Winston smiled. "He and I were thinking a secret wedding would be best, as soon as possible. How does tomorrow sound?"

Bee blinked. "Tomorrow?" Marrying Winston immediately sounded like a wonderful idea, especially if it meant she could keep kissing him. But all of her insecurities rose up to swamp her. She was too thin, too weak, too boyish.

Not good enough, echoed Malorie's voice in her head. *No gentleman would want a wife like you.*

She ducked her head to avoid Winston's gaze. "Are you sure? Look at me. I'm—"

"Beautiful." He kissed her forehead. *"Alive."* He kissed her temple. "Courageous." One cheek. "Resilient." The other cheek. He let go of her with one arm so that he could gently lift her chin until she was looking at him. "The only girl I've wanted to marry since I was six years old." He brushed a feather-light kiss on the tip of her nose. "Shall I go on? Fierce." Kiss. "Independent." Kiss. "Amazing in every possible way." He pressed his lips to hers, and Bee decided that this was the best, most convincing argument she'd ever received.

"Tomorrow sounds perfect," she said breathlessly. "But what do I wear? I only have your mother's dresses."

Winston laughed and pulled her close again. "Haven't I told you that I don't care what you wear? I would have married you in the trousers you wore yesterday. That's not what it's about, Bee. I love you, and I never want to let you out of my arms again."

CHAPTER 25

Warmth spread through Bee, and she closed her eyes, snuggling into his side. "I love you, too. You've always been the best thing in my life, you know that? Even when I was goading you into sparring with me. I missed you horribly when you were at Oxford, and even more after I left home."

The door to the drawing room opened, startling Bee, but Winston's arms remained too firmly in place for her to jump back. Her cheeks burned at the thought of being caught in a compromising position, but she heard only laughter in Miss Hilton's voice.

"So it's settled, then?"

"Yes, she's agreed to marry me tomorrow." Bee had never heard Winston sound so happy.

"Tomorrow? You'd best start making arrangements."

Winston's arms reluctantly loosened, and Bee sat back. Her best friend grinned at her before getting to his feet. "I'll see you at dinner." He excused himself and left the women alone.

Miss Hilton seemed to think that the events of the morning had been too strenuous and required extra rest. Bee submitted to another cup of tea before being bundled into bed for a nap. There was no way she could sleep, not now. She was too full of happy flutters over Winston and nervous flutters over wondering what Papa intended to do about Malorie. But she lay obediently in bed, resting. An hour later, Miss Hilton peeked in and, seeing her awake, ushered in a footman with a large trunk. A trunk Bee recognized.

"Your father sent this over," the governess said.

"That's the case I sent to town with Papa." Bee swung her legs out of bed. "The servants were going to have it all unpacked and ready for me to make my arrival easier."

She crossed to the trunk and unlatched it. Across the top

lay folded a brand new gown of sprigged muslin trimmed with tiny ribbon rosettes. Bee frowned. This dress wasn't hers; she'd never worn anything like it. Then she remembered Malorie writing ahead to place an order with the modiste so that the gowns would be ready for a fitting as soon as they arrived. They must have been delivered to the town house right around the time that Papa was called home with terrible news.

Bee lifted the dress from the trunk and laid it out on the bed. There was another new gown in lavender, and a third in sage green jaconet. Beneath those were the morning dresses Bee remembered, and piles of shawls and stockings and gloves. She stared at it all, stunned. Then she laughed.

"I guess I won't have to get married in one of Lady Rowland's gowns after all."

***

The wedding was a tiny, quiet affair. The minister stood before the hearth in the drawing room, and Bee and Winston faced him. Bee wore the sprigged muslin, which was loose but not horribly so. Papa and Miss Hilton were witnesses. Winston looked more handsome than ever, and Bee couldn't stop smiling.

Winston had decided not to say a word to his parents but to let them be surprised when they arrived in town for the season. Though it seemed cruel to make them wait, Bee didn't want word of her survival to get out. Papa had hired the Bow Street Runners to look into Malorie's murder attempts. They'd been to the house to meet with Bee once already, and she'd given as much detail as she could about the vegetable stall where she'd stolen the apple. Bee hadn't heard yet whether the owner of the stall had admitted to anything. She suspected the Runners were interviewing the huntsmen employed at Eston Hall as well, but no one would tell her much. Everyone insisted that she not worry and focus solely on eating and regaining her strength.

Less than a month later, Lord and Lady Rowland arrived in town. Lady Rowland went so white when she saw Bee that Winston called for smelling salts, but instead of fainting, his mother dissolved into tears and fell upon Bee's neck, sobbing. That, of course, led to tears from everyone else, and it took a full hour and several pots of tea before they were all recovered.

Winston's parents were perfectly willing to remain at home and maintain Bee's secrecy, and they had a cozy little family party in the Mayfair town house for that first week until Bee's father arrived in the drawing room one day.

He looked sad and tired. "The Runners have Malorie under magical guard. I'll travel with them as far as Newgate to see her safely locked away." He gestured to the window.

A glance outside showed an official-looking coach parked before the house. The curtain at one of the coach windows pulled aside, revealing Malorie's lovely and bitter face.

"She's right there?" Lady Rowland gasped. "Outside our house?"

"I… I wanted to give Bianca the chance to…" Papa shrugged, floundering.

To ask Malorie why she'd done it? To offer forgiveness? To put this chapter of her life behind her?

Bee didn't know what he intended, but she moved closer to the window of the drawing room all the same. Winston went with her, his arm firmly supportive at her waist. The motion must have drawn Malorie's gaze, because her eyes locked on Bee from her seat in the coach, and her glare turned poisonous. Bianca felt no need to speak to Malorie again or to subject herself to her stepmother's venom, and she was far from prepared to offer forgiveness. But she needed to see her, to reassure herself that Malorie was only a woman—a sad, spiteful woman, but a woman nonetheless—not an evil witch from a children's story. And she needed Malorie to see her, to see that she was alive and strong and ready to thrive and be happy.

"Thank you, Papa," she said, stepping back from the window and turning to her father.

"You'll be safe now, snowflake." He took her hand. "I'm sorry I ever brought her home with me. I'm sorry I didn't see what was going on."

"It's done, Papa." Bee leaned in to kiss his cheek. "We're all alive and well." She nestled into Winston's embrace as her father left the house.

Now that it was safe to go out about town, Miss Hilton returned to her niece's family, and Lady Rowland took great pleasure in introducing Bee to her vast acquaintance as "my daughter, Mrs. Graham." Lady Rowland was every bit the mother Bee had always wanted, though Bee still occasionally missed Nurse, who had loved her first and longest. For her part, Bee found her first London Season to be more enjoyable even than she'd hoped. The social obligations were as tedious as predicted, but being introduced to the *ton* by Lady Rowland was infinitely preferable to how it would have gone with Malorie. Winston kept his promise to show her everything she'd been wishing to see, and he kept coming up with new places to go, just so that they could drive out together and

CHAPTER 25

avoid morning callers.

One pair of callers, however, Bee was eager to see. Lord Larkwell came one morning with Miss Sally Clarke, who kissed Bee's cheeks and hugged her tightly.

"I have heard more gossip about you than I know what to do with," she said to Bee, "but I can't tell you how glad I am that you're alive."

Bee grinned. "Neither can I."

They all laughed. Sally wouldn't be satisfied until she heard Bee's whole story, and only then did she announce her own good news: she was soon to become Lady Larkwell.

She blushed becomingly as she said it, with a sidelong smile at Lord Larkwell, who sat in a chair nearby. He beamed at her dreamily before turning to Bee.

"You were right, of course, Mrs. Graham," he said. "Your friend Miss Clarke was *exactly* the lady I was looking for."

She laughed and insisted that he call her Bee. "Sally is my dearest friend, after all, which makes you practically family. It is a shame I wasn't able to introduce you properly last Season." She grinned mischievously. "But I did my best."

"You did your—what can you mean?"

"We met months after you… that is…"

"After I disappeared? Yes, I know. But *you* ought to know that if I'd really wanted the reticule, you'd never have gotten it back. I'm not such a clumsy thief as all that."

The shock on their faces was all that Bee had hoped as they spluttered their surprise.

"The reticule—how did you—?"

"*You?* That was you the whole time?"

Bee laughed and shrugged. "I had a promise to keep, and it was too good an opportunity to pass up."

They had a good laugh over it, and the two couples saw each other often throughout the Season. Bee was Sally's attendant at their wedding in May, and she waved them off on their honeymoon with a smile that hurt her cheeks.

Not long after, Lord and Lady Rowland began talking of returning to the country soon. Privately, Bee asked Winston if he minded staying in town a bit longer.

"Of course not, Honeybee. And we don't need to go home to Pinehurst at all if you'd rather not. I haven't forgotten our plans to see France and the West Indies and everything in between."

"I think we might delay that a bit too. Tell me what you think of this idea…"

Chapter 26

June had come. Winston's parents had returned to Pinehurst a week ago. The sunny morning was stretching on toward noon as Bee paced the drawing room nervously.

"Do you think they'll come?"

Winston came up behind her and wrapped his arms around her waist, halting her movement. "Davy said he'd bring them. Don't worry."

He'd gone out the previous day to find the young artist to implement the first step in Bee's plan. She'd wanted to go with him, but they'd agreed eventually that it was best if Winston delivered the message himself. It was a simple request: that the seven boys come to Mayfair to see Whites and have dinner.

Bee couldn't imagine they'd turn down a free meal, but she didn't know how they'd respond to the rest of her proposal, or to the revelation that she wasn't, in fact, a boy.

A few minutes later, there was a commotion in the corridor, and a footman opened the door for the visitors. Seven dirty boys, some of whom had grown an inch or more since she'd last seen them, trooped into the drawing room, looking around slack-jawed in awe.

"Glad you could come," Winston said with a smile. "You

probably remember me well enough, but I'd like to introduce my wife, Bianca Graham."

Bee felt everyone's eyes on her. The younger boys' faces were all openly curious, but Grim's expression was closed off, and even Davy's was hard to read. She smiled nervously. "Winston promised you dinner, and we'll get to that soon, but first I wanted to make you all an offer." She glanced at Winston, whose smile was all the encouragement she needed. "We'd like to adopt you. All of you. Become your guardians. You'd have clean clothes and plenty of food—"

Nearly all the boys started talking at once, and it took a minute for everyone to quiet down.

"It's up to you, of course," Bee said when the hubbub had subsided. "We'll feed you today regardless of what you choose. But I do hope you'll consider it. You'd have lessons, but not just the boring ones. You can study art," she cut a glance at Davy, "or magic," her eyes moved to Jack, "and I can guarantee all the bedtime stories you want." Johnny's blue eyes widened when she smiled at him.

"That's good an' all, but where's Whites?" Squid asked. "Doodles said 'e'd be here."

"*She's* Whites, you bottle-headed nodcock," Grim grumbled.

Bee bit her lip, then slipped into her old cant way of speaking with a grin. "'E ain't bottle-headed. Ain't nothin' wrong with asking, 'specially since 'e were expecting a cull, not a toff lady." The twins' jaws practically hit the floor, and Squid looked like a light breeze would knock him down. Bee looked at Grim. In her normal voice, she asked, "How long have you known?"

"Since the day 'e came." Grim nodded at Winston. "Ain't nobody should look at a boy the way 'e looked at you."

"Like you were the sun," Davy added softly, "and 'e ain't had nothing but rain without you."

Bee looked at him in surprise. She turned to Winston, whose ears were pink. He rubbed the back of his neck.

"I may not have hidden my feelings very well." He grimaced.

Jack shuffled his feet and scowled up at Winston. "If that's so, I shouldn't'a hit you."

It wasn't much of an apology by most standards, but Bee could see it was genuine. She looked between the boy and Winston. "You never told me Jack hit you."

Winston nodded. "Solid punch, too."

"It should be," Bee laughed. "I taught him." She winked at Jack. "Well, it's all out in the open now. I do hope you'll forgive me for lying, and I want to thank you for giving me a place with you. You all saved my life just as much as Winston did that day." She moved to perch on the edge of the sofa and tried not to fiddle with the cushions. "I know it's a big decision, but will you consider our offer? You've been like brothers to me, and I'd like to treat you all as family."

Johnny's angelic curls danced as he tilted his head and eyed her thoughtfully. "Could I call you Mum? On'y, I never 'ad one o' them, an' they sound nice."

Bee's heart was fit to burst. "Of course you can. Or you can call me Bee—that's what most of the family calls me."

"An' you're serious about magic lessons?" Jack asked. "And boxing?"

"I'll teach you myself," Winston said. "We can start tomorrow."

They were interrupted by a maid announcing that nuncheon was served. The boys looked at Bee, confused. "Food," she said. "We'll eat now, and if you'd like, you can stay the afternoon and have dinner later."

It took all of Winston's calm authority and Bee's persuasion to keep the boys from gorging themselves. She had to remind them again and again of how tiny her meals had needed to be when Winston first brought her home. Finally, to distract them, she suggested that they return to the drawing room and she'd tell them how she'd ended up on the streets of London in the first place. They got comfortable, the boys flopped any which way onto the furniture, and Bee cringed inwardly at the extra work for the servants having to get the dirt out. But they were her boys, and she was glad they were there. The story didn't take long to tell, or it wouldn't have if there had been fewer interruptions. When she'd finished, Bee asked again if any of the boys had decided whether to stay with them.

Johnny agreed immediately. A mother who told bedtime stories was just what the six-year-old needed, and he already knew that Bee told good ones. Jack and Squid accepted the offer too—Jack couldn't pass up the chance to learn magic, and Squid admitted to wanting as much food as he could eat.

"What's your Christian name?" Bee asked him. "Squid can't be it."

"Nah." Squid kicked his dangling foot against the side of the chair he was sprawled across. "It's Sam."

"I hope you don't mind if we call you Sam, then."

Squid shrugged but didn't complain.

Davy also accepted. Bee knew he'd love art lessons with the masters, and she intended to introduce him to Lord and Lady Larkwell as soon as possible.

The twins waffled a bit—lessons sounded less appealing, but food was an obvious draw. When Bee told them that they'd spend a good part of the year in the country where they could learn to ride horses and have the run of two estates, with a

CHAPTER 26

forest to adventure in, they agreed to come.

"But you'll have to tell me your names too," she said. "I can't always call you 'the twins,' particularly if one of you gets into trouble when the other doesn't."

"We always get into trouble together," they assured her with matching grins on their freckled faces. But they told her their names: Robert and Ryan.

"What about you, Grim?" Bee asked. He'd been silent the whole time, watching inscrutably.

"No, thanks," he said quietly. "It's a good chance for this lot, growing up like toffs an' having a real family, like. But I'm old enough to get an honest job, an' if I only 'ave myself to worry about, I reckon I'll be a'right."

He met Bee's eyes squarely, and she imagined that she saw a burden lifting from his shoulders as she took on the care of the younger boys, freeing him to step up into a different kind of responsibility and manhood on his own. She was sad that he wouldn't be coming with them, but she was proud of him too.

"The offer doesn't expire," she said softly. "And if you ever need anything at all, you're welcome here."

Grim nodded.

Grim stayed for dinner before heading back alone to the attic that was all his now. On his way out, Bee made sure to introduce him to Mrs. Stephens, the housekeeper, so that if he ever came to the house while the family was in the country, she would know him and get him whatever help he needed.

After dinner, a bath was filled and refilled in one of the downstairs parlors while a footman attempted to clean the boys up. A servant had been dispatched to Winston's tailor as soon as they'd known which boys were staying, and he'd returned with six nightshirts in various sizes, with the promise that trousers and shirts would be delivered by morning. Bee hardly recognized the boys once they were clean, in new nightshirts, their hair still damp. Squid—Sam—was actually a lighter blond than she'd thought, and the twins' red hair practically glowed. Bee told them a bedtime story while they all sat by the fire in one of the spare bedrooms, then she and Winston bundled them off into bed. There weren't enough rooms for the boys to avoid sharing, but two or three to a bed was significantly better than eight in a tiny attic, sleeping on the floor.

When she'd said goodnight to all of them, and told Johnny one last silly story, Bee retired to the room she shared with Winston. She sat by the fire, overwhelmed by the day. Her idea had been successful: her boys had a home, a family, and a promising future. But as she slowly unpinned her growing hair and ran her fingers through it, she realized that there were a great many things she hadn't prepared for. Winston came in then, closing the door and removing his boots before padding over to her. His hand made slow circles on her back as he bent over to kiss her head.

"Today was brilliant," he said. "The attorney's already working on guardianship papers." He caught sight of her worried frown. "What's wrong? Are you having second thoughts? I know you've said you wanted to travel rather than be stuck at home raising children."

"It's not that." Bee shook her head. "We'll travel the world eventually, and for now we'll take holidays—I've been thinking Brighton would be nice, and I'd love to see the lake district..." She shook her head again to bring herself back from the places she'd imagined visiting for so long. "And we'll visit them together as a family, never leaving anyone behind."

"Then what is it? I thought your plan came together perfectly."

"It did," Bee said, looking up at him, "but there's so much I forgot to think of. Who will teach them? Do you think Miss Hilton could handle them? Or maybe Mr. Turbot would be available? Could they, together, manage six boys who've never had to sit still in their lives? And how are we ever to get them all to Pinehurst? Even if we bought a wagon, we'd need more space!"

Winston laughed and drew her to her feet. He pulled her close, and just the warmth of his arms around her calmed her racing mind.

"Slow down, Honeybee," he murmured, resting his cheek against her hair. "We don't have to solve every potential problem tonight. We have a wonderful family—an *enormous*, wonderful family. All we can do is love each other, love them, and take each day as it comes."

Bee smiled and hugged Winston tighter, then tipped her head up for a kiss. "I can handle that."

***

Join my mailing list at elizaprokopovits.com for new releases, updates, and more!

***

Want more magic in Regency England? Read on for chapter 1 of *Her Enchanted Tower*, a retelling of "Rapunzel."

REGENCY MAGIC FAERIE TALES
BOOK 5

HER ENCHANTED TOWER

ELIZA PROKOPOVITS

Her Enchanted Tower: Chapter 1

Catherine Whitmer was bored. Not just today or because it was raining. Every day. Her life was stiflingly dull.

Mama repeatedly assured her that all young ladies of a certain class spent their days embroidering and painting and practicing their music. Mama always followed that with an arched brow and, "You're quite lucky, you know, Kitty. Many ladies have no access to the quantity of books you read."

Catherine didn't doubt that Mama was right about the books, but she couldn't help feeling that she was missing out on a great deal of life. Surely other young ladies had better things to fill their time with than histories and geographies or even novels. Not that Mama let Catherine read novels often, but sometimes as a special treat she'd bring one home from the lending library when she'd been to the market. Books of magic were nearly as good as novels—they were a good bit more useful than the biography of William the Conqueror that sat forgotten on Catherine's lap, at any rate.

Catherine sighed and leaned her elbow on the tiny, narrow windowsill, one finger holding her place in the book while her attention drifted. The gray sky she'd woken up to had let loose, and now a dull, steady rain fell. The drab, dreary world outside her window felt like too accurate a reflection of her life. No one would be out in this weather, and like so many times over the past six years, Catherine could easily pretend that she and Mama were the only two people in the world.

Eventually, the rain tapered off. A pale, weak sun shone faintly through the dissipating clouds. Catherine placed her bookmark and set the biography aside. She loved the way the garden looked after rain, and this would be the perfect time to try out her new watercolors. She gathered her papers, easel, paints, and a blanket to sit on before tying an apron over her morning dress. Wrapping a worn green shawl around her shoulders, she gathered everything else into her arms and descended the winding staircase that carried her through each open level of the tower. Mama, her humming blending with the whirring of her spinning wheel, didn't look up as Catherine passed through.

"I'm going outside to paint," Catherine called.

"Dry off the bench first," Mama advised, still not looking up.

Catherine wound down another three levels to the kitchen, where she wrangled the heavy wooden door open without dropping anything. She paused on the wooden steps outside to breathe. The air smelled so fresh and clean and full of life, and the brightening sun glittered on the water that dripped from every leaf and twig and gleamed on each flagstone. The garden was barely recognizable in such a magical light. It looked fae and enchanted and full of possibility. Catherine could forget, as she carried her supplies to the bench in the farther corner, that she'd spent hours weeding the vegetable beds just yesterday.

The bench was as wet as everything else, of course. Catherine carefully lay her easel and paint set on the ground to free up one hand, which she held open and flat over the bench. She murmured a spell-word and couldn't stifle the giggle that came when the warm air rushed from her hand to dry the stone surface. This spell tickled, and she could only do it for so long before she had to stop and itch her palm. It was enough, however, and she laid the folded blanket on the bench to sit on. In a moment, she had her easel set up with paper, paints, and brushes at the ready. She'd forgotten to bring out a cup of water, so she skipped back inside to get one, then looked around to choose a subject for her painting.

Her eyes fell on the tower. The rain had made the stones darker so that it looked almost sinister as it loomed over the sprawling garden. It was an old round tower from the time of the Norman invasion—hence her choice of biography, however tedious—with a few broken bits of wall jutting jaggedly from the base. There had been more to the old building, but it had been unsalvageable ruins when Mama had first moved in, and the crumbled walls now formed part of the boundary of the garden, which was an asymmetrical not-quite-square. Catherine had always found the tower to be a rather romantic home, especially when she was in a gothic mood after reading a good novel, and she wondered how many people were lucky enough to live in a stone ruin. It wasn't easy to reclaim or maintain a tower like this. One needed a good deal of either money or magic to make it livable. Mama used magic.

Catherine began painting, letting the tower fill one side of her paper while the lilac walk and vegetable beds spread over the rest of the page. Birdsong and rainwater dripping from the leaves of the trees beyond the garden formed the background music to her art, and Catherine began to sing along. Singing to fill the silent loneliness was something she'd been doing for years, and she absently made up a song about rain in May.

She was on the fifth nonsense verse when a sound from

the trees startled her. Whirling around, she froze, her mouth still open but the song choked off. Standing in the shadows beneath the trees stood a man and a horse. The horse blew again, and Catherine recognized the sound that had alarmed her, but she couldn't tear her eyes from the man standing at the horse's head.

He was somewhere between tall and short, perhaps a few inches taller than she was, and he wore an olive coat over tan breeches and black riding boots. The fabric clung to him as though he'd been caught in the tail end of the downpour. His cheeks reddened as she stared at him. "Forgive me for startling you. Your singing... I could have listened all day."

"Oh," was all Catherine managed. Her face felt hot, and she didn't know what to do with her hands. She twisted them in her apron as she glanced around the garden.

"You enjoy painting?"

He spoke as if he were grasping for a subject of conversation. Perhaps he'd been taught to avoid uncomfortable silences and to fill them with pleasant chatter. He couldn't be as nervous as she was.

"I'm... I'm not supposed to talk to strangers." Catherine's eyes fell on the tower, and she was glad Mama's window faced the other direction. *Not supposed to talk to strangers.* What an understatement. This man was the first person aside from Mama that she'd seen in six years.

A smile pulled at the gentleman's mouth, and Catherine watched his unexceptional features turn into something wondrous, full of humor and friendliness. "That's easy enough to rectify," he said, removing his hat and bowing. "I am Lord Henry Stanton, at your service."

Catherine found herself smiling in turn. She rose and

curtsied as Mama had taught her. "Catherine Whitmer. It's a pleasure to make your acquaintance."

"The pleasure's all mine, Miss Whitmer."

Catherine cringed at the name. "Oh, no, that won't do," she blurted without thinking, causing his eyes to widen in surprise. "That makes me sound stuffy and old like Mama."

He grinned and ran a hand through his hair. It was a medium brown, as unremarkable as the rest of him, but Catherine liked the way it ruffled messily. "What shall I call you, then?"

She hesitated. It wasn't the thing for a stranger to call one by one's Christian name, however much one might want to like them already. But his countenance was so open and genuine, she couldn't help trusting him. "I've always wanted to be Kate. Mama calls me Kitty, but it's not the same at all."

"No, I suppose not," he agreed. "Kate it is, then, and you may call me Henry." As they'd talked, he and his horse had drawn nearer to the garden wall. He leaned his hip against it now and studied Catherine. "So, Kate, now that we're not strangers, tell me: do you enjoy painting?"

Catherine pressed her lips together to keep her smile in check. Why did her cheeks feel like they were glowing? Henry was not as handsome as the heroes in the novels she'd read. His nose was a bit too big, and his jaw wasn't chiseled, and his shoulders didn't strain against the seams of his coat. His eyes were a vague, muddy shade she couldn't label. But his face was pleasant, and his smile warm, and his eyes held a hint of laughter that drew her in.

"I do," she said. "I enjoy sketching with charcoal as well, but watercolor seemed more suited to the scenery."

"Indeed, water is quite the theme today." Henry chuckled. "I ventured out too soon, when what I'd thought was the shower ending was only a lull."

"You ought to go home and change before you catch cold."

"I really ought to," he agreed. "A damp coat isn't the most pleasant thing on a cool day."

"I should think not," Catherine agreed, though she wouldn't have minded him staying a bit longer. Talking to someone besides Mama was refreshing in a way she'd entirely forgotten.

He smiled at her again and bowed, replaced his hat, and swung himself into the saddle. "It was a pleasure meeting you, Kate."

"Yes," Catherine said softly as he turned his horse and rode back into the trees. She stared after him long after he was gone.

***

By the time Catherine had put away her paints and gone inside for dinner, she had a completed watercolor and had long since stopped blushing. Mama's dark eyes examined the artwork critically. They were pretty eyes, with lovely, long, dark lashes, only hidden behind thick spectacles. Mama's thin lips pursed as she pointed out a few places where Catherine's technique could improve. Catherine took the instruction meekly, as it was no more than she'd expected. Mama treated everything as an opportunity for improvement, refusing to settle for less than perfection in any regard. She dismissed Catherine to put away her art supplies, urging her to hurry back down to set the table for dinner.

In her room at the top of the tower, Catherine took a moment to tidy away everything she'd gotten out. Mama was fastidious about housekeeping as well, and with such a small living space, Catherine couldn't deny that it was nice to have everything in its place and out of the way. Before she rejoined Mama in the kitchen, she paused by her window, gazing out over the garden and trees to the distant hills that shaded purple in the sunset. She slowly untied her apron, letting her mind wander for a moment. Somewhere out there, there were people. People who went about their lives with no idea that Catherine existed. Except one. Somewhere out there was a specific person named Henry who called her Kate and liked hearing her sing.

Catherine wrenched her mind away from these musings. She couldn't let on to Mama that anything different had happened today. She hung the apron on its hook on the wall and hurried down the stairs. Mama sliced a loaf of bread as Catherine got out plates and cups. As she maneuvered through the small space, trading places with Mama in their familiar dance of meal preparation, she noticed again how short Mama was, a few inches shorter than Catherine. Mama's long, dark hair was twisted at the nape of her neck in a severe knot. Catherine wondered if a softer style would suit Mama better, perhaps make her cheekbones appear less rigid, her chin less sharp. But soft was not the first word Catherine would use to describe Mama. Precise and perfectionistic, yes, and loving, in her own strict way. Catherine never doubted that Mama cared more for her than for anything in the world. But there were old secrets that made Mama afraid, and whenever Catherine came too close to asking about them, she was sent straight to bed.

Mama set the last serving dish on the table and sat across from Catherine. "What are you thinking of, Kitty? You look miles away."

"Not miles," Catherine said lightly. "I was wondering if you would let me try a new hairstyle on you, on a day when you don't have errands in the village. And I was thinking about how I might paint you, if you were ever to sit for me."

Mama's smile was faint but present. "I haven't done my hair in any other way since I was your age and attending balls in town."

Catherine itched to ask why *she* wasn't allowed to go to town, or even to attend any local assemblies, if Mama had been taken about by *her* mother. But that was a certain way to be sent to bed without finishing dinner, and Catherine was hungry.

When dinner was over and the dishes washed and put away, Catherine retired to her room, ostensibly to read for a short while by rushlight before going to sleep. But she didn't bother with the light. She used a spell that lit a flame in her palm so that she could see to find her nightgown, but she extinguished it quickly and got dressed in the dark. She slid between the sheets and pulled the wool coverlet up to her chin. Now, alone in the dark, she allowed her mind to wander again. Instantly, the charming stranger was before her eyes, leaning against the garden wall as he called her Kate. Warmth filled her belly as she remembered how his face lit up when he smiled and how his hair fell messily after he'd run his fingers through it. She wondered what color his eyes actually were. She wondered if, wherever he was, he was thinking of her, and whether she'd ever see him again.

***

Pick up your copy of *Her Enchanted Tower* now to continue reading!

Also By Eliza Prokopovits

Ember and Twine

Jewels and Dragons

The Thunderstone Theft

Regency Magic Faerie Tales
   Her Fae Secret
   The Beast's Magician
   Her Forgotten Sea
   Her Cursed Apple

About the Author

Eliza Prokopovits (pro-COP-o-vits) is a writer and knitting designer. She is obsessed with books, yarn, and dark chocolate. She lives in Pennsylvania with her husband, two boys, and aging goldendoodle.

Printed in Great Britain
by Amazon